After pushing off from the dry adobe wall, Quinn began the stalk.

His left hand brushed against his deputy badge, his right shifted his Colt pistol, making sure the gun was loose in the holster. A breeze crept across the street, ruffling the woman's veil. Quinn itched to rip the cloth away. Back stiff, the woman lifted her skirts again to step over a pile of manure. Before her foot touched ground, Quinn had her by the elbow. His grip wasn't gentle. No way would he lose the Veiled Widow.

She gasped. Her arm jerked.

He tightened his hold.

"Ouch. Let me go." She tugged hard, stumbling to the side.

"I don't believe I will, Ma'am. You're coming with me."

NANCY J. FARRIER resides in Arizona with her husband, son, and four daughters. She is the author of numerous articles and short stories. Her days are busy with home-schooling her daughters. Nancy feels called to share her faith with others through her writing. Readers voted her "favorite new author" for 2001.

HEARTSONG PRESENTS

Books by Nancy J. Farrier
HP415—Sonoran Sunrise
HP449—An Ostrich a Day

Sonoran
Star

Nancy J. Farrier

Heartsong Presents

To Marie and Ellen, sisters extraordinaire.

A note from the author:
*I love to hear from my readers! You may correspond with me
by writing:*   **Nancy J. Farrier**
                  Author Relations
                  PO Box 719
                  Uhrichsville, OH 44683

ISBN 1-58660-531-3

SONORAN STAR

All Scripture quotations are taken from the King James Version of
the Bible.

All of the characters and events in this book are fictitious. Any
resemblance to actual persons, living or dead, or to actual events
is purely coincidental.

Cover illustration by Kay Salem.

PRINTED IN THE U.S.A.

one

Quinn Kirby finished digging the splinter from his thumb, wiped the blade on his pants, snapped the pocketknife shut, and pushed it into his pocket. The thrum of horses' hooves, accompanied by the rattle of the stage, echoed down the quiet street. He turned to the right and leaned his shoulder against the rough-hewn boards of the mercantile. Glancing down to make sure his deputy badge still shone from last night's polishing, he continued his patient wait for the stage.

Every day was the same. The afternoon stage would arrive, and Quinn would be waiting—waiting for her, so he could arrest her. He knew one day the thief, known as the Veiled Widow, would show up here in Tucson. When she did, he'd be ready. Quinn wasn't afraid of arresting a woman. From the reports coming in over the wires, the Widow was getting bolder all the time.

Her modus operandi—he rolled the fancy police term around in his mind, fighting the faint smile that touched his lips—involved showing up in a town and acting helpless. She targeted older, well-to-do gentlemen. She stayed long enough to get the gentleman to cough up a tidy sum, then she disappeared. No one would hear about her for weeks until she came out of hiding to strike again. Her appetite for wealth seemed to be growing. In the last few months, she'd struck with alarming frequency.

The stage rattled to a stop in a cloud of dust that settled to the ground in a slow waltz. White lather flecked the horses' harness straps. Quinn straightened. Eight weeks ago the Widow had robbed and wounded a man in Texas. She seemed to be working her way west. To Quinn's way of thinking, that made Tucson a likely destination. He was here to make sure she didn't carry out her manipulations on any of the fine citizens of the town he'd sworn to protect.

The driver climbed down from the top of the stagecoach. His bones creaked as loud as the stage. He opened the door, stepped to the side, and held out his hand. Quinn brushed the handle of his pistol. The driver wouldn't be helping a man from the coach.

The sight of a small foot encased in a black shoe made Quinn's heart accelerate. Muscles tense, he flexed his fingers, and he held his breath. The woman climbed out, one hand holding her dark green skirt up so she wouldn't trip. A dainty matching hat trimmed with a pheasant feather and no veil perched atop her gray-streaked hair. Mrs. Baker. She and her husband must be getting home from their trip to Albuquerque to visit their daughter. Lena Baker smiled at the driver. Richard Baker climbed from the coach and took his wife's arm to help her to the side of the street. A young man, thin and gawky, clambered from the stage, grabbing the door just in time to keep from falling in the dust.

Quinn watched as the young man righted himself and turned to help catch the luggage being lowered to the ground. Some of the tension drained away. He'd had such hopes that she would be on the stage today. In fact, he woke this morning with the feeling that he would arrest her today. He could almost picture the black veil covering her face, her trim figure decked in a black traveling dress, slender long-fingered hands holding the skirt up in a delicate manner as she stepped down. Quinn jumped. He wasn't just thinking this; he was seeing her. The lanky youth finished helping the woman, came close to falling again as he offered her his arm, then reddened as she turned and walked away from the stagecoach straight toward the elderly Mr. Ash, one of the richest men in town.

After pushing off from the dry adobe wall, Quinn began the stalk. His left hand brushed against his deputy badge, his right shifted his Colt pistol, making sure the gun was loose in the holster. A breeze crept across the street, ruffling the woman's veil. Quinn itched to rip the cloth away. Back stiff, the woman lifted her skirts again to step over a pile of manure. Before her foot touched ground, Quinn had her by the elbow. His grip wasn't gentle. No way would he lose the Veiled Widow.

She gasped. Her arm jerked.

He tightened his hold.

"Ouch. Let me go." She tugged hard, stumbling to the side.

"I don't believe I will, Ma'am. You're coming with me."

She turned her head toward him. "I will not. I don't even know you. Now, if you'll let me go, I'm expecting someone."

Quinn shook his head. "You are despicable. You haven't even been in town two minutes and you already have your victim picked out." He wrapped his hand tightly around her slender arm.

"If you don't release me right now, I'll have the authorities called."

Lifting his hat with his free hand, Quinn smiled. "I am the authority, Ma'am. Deputy Quinn Kirby at your service."

"What?" She stopped struggling. The stage passengers stared as they waited in the shade of the building.

"Let's go, Widow. I have some mighty fine accommodations for you."

"Widow? Accommodations? I don't know what you're talking about. Did my cousin send you?"

Fine dust curled up around their legs as Quinn marched her down the street. He had to admit she was good. From her tone, he could almost believe she had no idea why he was arresting her. No wonder so many lawmen and businessmen had succumbed to her charms. "I don't know your cousin.

I'm here to arrest you for robbery."

"What?" Despite his grip, she stopped in the middle of the street. Wrenching her arm to the side and getting loose, she staggered back.

Quinn lunged at her before she could get her footing. This woman was one slippery character. He misjudged the distance and smacked into her. They both tumbled onto the roadway. Quinn twisted in midfall so he wouldn't drop on top of her. His shoulder landed with a splat in a fresh pile of manure.

The Widow fell hard beside him. Her hair tumbled loose. The hat with the veil attached dropped to one side. Quinn found himself gazing into the most incredible hazel eyes he'd ever seen—green, dotted with flecks of yellow, bordered by a ring of darker green. He forgot the horse manure. He couldn't remember why he wanted to arrest her. All he could think of was how much he wanted to stay here and look into those amazing eyes.

She blinked. Her lips twitched. A picture flashed through Quinn's mind of him lying in the street with horse manure dripping from his cheek. No wonder she wanted to laugh. Before he found himself chuckling with a known criminal, Quinn leapt to his feet. He offered her a hand up. She accepted and turned her face to the left as she rose. All humor faded from her beautiful eyes.

"My hat." She started to bend over and pick it up.

Quinn jerked her to his side. "Oh, no, you don't. I'm not giving you a second chance to escape."

"Please, I'm not trying to escape. I need my veil." She continued to tilt her head to the side. Her peaches-and-cream complexion had a light sprinkle of pale freckles. Long, dark eyelashes brushed against her cheek as she blinked. Mahogany hair shone in the afternoon light despite a light coating of Arizona dust.

"Why do you want a veil? What are you trying to hide?"

Quinn wondered, then realized he'd spoken the words aloud. He caught her other arm and pulled her around. His eyes widened in surprise. On her left cheek, marring the perfection, was a star-shaped birthmark. The reddish-brown blemish covered a large portion of her cheek.

&

Kathleen O'Connor felt heat flush her face. Deputy Kirby stood gawking at her like the school kids had when she was a girl. That's why her parents had taken her out of school. The familiar taunts came flooding back. *"Hey, devil girl." "She's Satan's spawn."* The whisperings, the mothers who forced their children to the other side of the street when she passed by. The years of horror washed over her.

She flinched. Trying to free her hand, she longed to cover her cheek. The deputy held her tight. Dipping her face to the left, Kathleen did her best to hide her birthmark-stained cheek with her shoulder. *God, please, help me.*

Deputy Kirby released her left arm. She pivoted away from him. He bent down, picked up her hat and veil from the dirt, and knocked them against his leg. Then he handed them to her. She wanted to cry. She didn't know why it mattered that this handsome man with his riveting blue-gray eyes wanted her face covered. She knew she wasn't fit for anyone to look at. Hadn't she been told that most of her life? Now she felt more shame than she'd known in years.

"Thank you." She nearly choked on the words.

Using her free hand to try to put the hat in place, Kathleen glanced at the deputy. His eyes glittered. He turned away and pulled her down the street. *Were those tears in his eyes? Does he feel sorry for me?*

"I don't need your pity."

"What?" He looked at her, his mouth set in a grim line.

"I said I don't need your pity. Just because I have a birthmark doesn't mean I'm evil."

They reached a small adobe building. The deputy opened a door that creaked in protest and pulled her inside. Kathleen blinked, trying to adjust to the dimness.

Kicking the door closed, the deputy motioned to the desk in one corner. "Leave your bag on the desk." He gave her a long look. "I don't pity you for the mark on your cheek. I pity you for the way of life you've chosen."

"My way of life?" Kathleen gaped. "Exactly what do you know about me?"

He snorted. "I've been following your career for months. I knew you'd turn up in Tucson eventually. Criminal sorts tend to find their way here. You think you can hide out here or that we'll be easy marks. Well, it didn't work this time. I was ready for you."

He dragged her across the small room to a cell. The deputy pulled the door open, ushered her to the cell, and slammed the door shut behind her.

"What are you doing?" Kathleen had never felt such out-rage. "Why am I being locked in a jail cell? I demand you let me out of here. And I don't know why you called me a widow. I am not a widow."

"Then why are you wearing black?"

"My mother gave me her old mourning dress. She said it's sensible for travel."

The deputy stepped away and hung the ring of keys on a nail near the cluttered desk. He hooked his thumbs in his belt loops, turned to face her, and relaxed his slim frame against the wall. "Don't think you can fool me. I know your type. You think you can shed a few tears and a man will do exactly what you want. Well, this man won't. You can cry all you want, and it won't do you any good."

Kathleen's mouth dropped open. "I've never in my life done that. I have no idea what you're talking about. I'm not a widow. I'm not a thief. I came to Tucson to visit my cousin.

You have no right to put me in this cell." Anger welled up inside. Who did he think he was, dragging her off to jail and accusing her of such ridiculous things? She glared at Quinn, using the practiced glare that always made her siblings cringe and do exactly what she'd asked of them.

Quinn appeared unaffected. Walking around the desk into the shadows beyond, he began to unbutton his shirt with a studied nonchalance. Kathleen turned her back, unwilling to watch. The rear door banged. She could hear water splashing as he cleaned the manure from his face and shoulder. She'd nearly laughed at the deputy when she'd first seen the manure splashed across his ear. Then, as now, the seriousness of her situation sobered her.

A feeling of helplessness wrapped around her. *God, what is going on here? Why am I in jail? I've never done anything against the law.*

The rough boards of the floor echoed like a hollow drum as the deputy clumped to the desk and pulled a different shirt from a peg on the wall. Kathleen tried not to watch. He had to be the handsomest man she'd ever laid eyes on. A slightly hooked nose added strength to his face. With his hat off, she could see the dark blond waves in his hair. She wondered if they gleamed even more in the sunlight than they did in the shadow. If looks were all a woman needed in a man, this one would make a fine husband.

What am I thinking? This man threw me in jail for no good reason, and all I can do is admire him. Kathleen wanted to kick herself. . .or maybe someone else.

After crossing to the front of the small cell, Kathleen wrapped her gloved fingers around the metal bars. She wondered how many truly desperate characters had gripped the bars this way before her. "I'd like to know how long you plan to keep me in here. My cousin's husband should be here any time to pick me up. What about my trunks? If someone takes them, you'll answer for it."

Deputy Kirby pulled out the chair, settled into the seat, and lifted his booted feet onto the scarred desk. "I'll send someone to fetch your trunks. We can store them for a time. Where you're going, you won't be needing them."

Waves of red-hot anger blurred Kathleen's vision. "Exactly where do you think I'll be going, besides my cousin's house?"

The deputy reached up and ran a hand through his unruly waves of hair, leaving them in even more disorder. "Why, Ma'am, I reckon you'll either be going to prison for a good, long time or swinging from a gallows when I'm done with you."

two

Kathleen could feel the blood draining from her face. Her grip tightened on the bars as her knees began to shake. She refused to show weakness before this lout who was bent on intimidating her. There must be some way to get him to see reason. Her cousin, Glorianna Sullivan, would be expecting her today. She'd sent a telegram at the last major town to let Glory know exactly what day she would arrive. *Lord, let someone tell Glory or her husband where I am. Please, help me.*

"I can't imagine the good townspeople in Tucson would allow you to hang an innocent woman." Kathleen fought a wave of dizziness at the thought of a hanging. "Our justice system is better than that."

"It is—if you're innocent." The deputy pulled a knife from his pocket and began to clean his fingernails as if he hadn't a care in the world. "Of course that fella in '73 claimed to be innocent too. Didn't do him any good." He paused, his light eyes gazing at her with the intensity of a hunter watching his prey. "The townsfolk hung him anyway, along with those three Mexican fellas who murdered Vicente Hernandez and his wife. Mrs. Hernandez was expecting their child. Folks were riled up real good. When folks out West get riled up about something, they're hard to reason with."

"Didn't anyone try to stop them? Didn't they get a fair trial?"

"Naw." Deputy Kirby's chair legs thumped on the floor as he sat up. He shoved the knife into his pocket and pulled out his pistol. "Old Milton Duffield tried to convince the boys to stop. He got a lump on the head for his troubles and slept through the whole lynching."

Nausea swept through Kathleen. Her legs felt as if they would give out. She leaned into the bars. "And where were you, Deputy? Didn't you try to stop them, or were you at the head of the mob?"

His eyes narrowed. "I'm here to uphold justice, not to take it in my own hands. If I'd been in town, I would have tried to stop them. So happens, I was out of town on business."

Pulling out a rag, he began to polish his pistol. "I reckon you'll come up before Doc Meyer in a couple of days."

"A doctor? I don't need a doctor. I need to get out of this jail."

He grinned, and his handsome face took on a boyish quality. "Oh, Doc Meyer isn't really a sawbones. He runs the drugstore. He's also our justice of the peace. He hears all the cases like yours, then decides what we should do."

Slipping his pistol into the holster, he strode across to her cell. "Ma'am, if you hold any tighter to those bars, you might leave marks on them. Why don't you have a seat on that bunk in there, and I'll run out and fetch you something to eat. There's one thing I know about riding the stage—you can build up a mighty thirst and hunger."

"I'm not hungry." Kathleen knew her dry throat could use something. "I would appreciate a drink, though, if you're sure it won't be wasted on someone who's to die so soon. I'd also like to speak to the sheriff."

"You'll have to talk mighty loud then. The sheriff is off with a couple of U.S. marshals on a manhunt up north." His eyes twinkled, and she found she couldn't turn away. "Now, Ma'am, I wouldn't have it said we mistreat our prisoners here in Tucson. I'll be back with your food in two twitches of a burro's ear."

She couldn't resist a parting shot. "I suppose lynching isn't considered mistreatment?"

He laughed. "No, Ma'am. Not when the criminal is as guilty as you."

The door creaked shut behind him. Kathleen could hear the scratch of the key turning in the lock. Tears burned in her eyes. What was going on here? She'd just come to Tucson to visit Glory and help her with the new baby. Everything seemed to be going wrong. The trip out here was miserable. The stage broke down twice, and the driver's stories of Apache attacks nearly scared her to death. Now, here she was so close to her destination but locked in a stinking jail on false charges, threatened with being hung. What next?

She released the bars. On legs that promised collapse at any moment, she made her way to the cot. She sank onto the dingy mattress, closing her eyes in relief at being able to sit. The next moment the smell of stale sweat and unidentified odors assaulted her. How could these people claim to be civilized when their jail was little better than a pigsty?

Slipping her gloved hands beneath her veil, Kathleen covered her face. Even through the gloves, she could feel the raised mark on her cheek, the mark that set her apart from others. She didn't understand why God had allowed her to be like this, but she tried not to question, only trust. Today, trust seemed too far from her grasp. She felt ugly, unwanted, and abandoned. All the feelings of hatred and fear directed at her from childhood seemed to crash over her now. She wept, silent tears dampening her travel-stained gloves.

❧

"Thank you, Señora Arvizu." Quinn smiled at the widow as she placed the plate of food in front of him. He inhaled the spicy scent of chilies. "I'll need another plate to take to the jail with me in a few minutes." The señora nodded, then squeezed her way past him to set a plate in front of Edward Fish, owner of Tucson's first steam-powered flour mill.

"Have you heard the good news?" Ed moved close to Quinn.

Scooping beans onto his fork with his folded tortilla, Quinn gave Ed a questioning look. "What news would that be?"

"The new schoolteachers have been hired and will arrive in a few weeks."

"Schoolteachers? They need two teachers to replace one?" Quinn shook his head, puzzled at the expense the town was taking on.

"Two female teachers." Edward's lips twitched with a rare smile. "Unattached teachers." He straightened and forked a bite into his mouth.

Quinn stared as he chewed. In this town unattached white females would be a novelty. "This is the stupidest thing I've ever heard of. Don't they realize this is a waste of money hiring women for the job? Unless they're the worst women in the world, they'll be married off within six months, and then the town will have to look for another teacher."

"That's true, but think of the advantage we single men have. Since I lost my wife, I've wanted to remarry. Maybe one of these young ladies will be just right for me. You can bet I'm willing to give them a chance."

"I still think the board should have given John Spring the raise he asked for or the assistant he needed."

"Well, if one of these ladies proves to be good marriage material, I'll be grateful to Spring for the uproar he caused. The school board was right. They can easily afford two female teachers for the one hundred twenty-five dollars a month they were paying him. His demand for an assistant or a raise of twenty-five dollars a month so he could hire his own assistant was ludicrous."

Quinn shoveled the last mouthful of beans into his mouth, swallowing before he continued. "I don't know. I think bringing women out here is a mistake. Not too long ago, we were having Apache attacks. This is man's territory and should remain that way until it's safe for women." He stood. "Besides, before I'd consider getting married, I'd have to meet a woman who's got plenty of spunk and courage." A vision of hazel eyes and a star-marked cheek floated through his mind. He pushed the thought away. He refused to be attracted to a criminal.

"Nice talking with you. I'd better get back to the jail and feed my charge." Before Ed could ask more, Quinn pushed his way through the crowded tables and collected a plate of food to take with him.

The outside air had cooled as the sun dropped low in the sky. Quinn drew in a deep breath, then wrinkled his nose. Despite washing, the scent of manure still clung to him. Then again, it could be the smell of the Tucson streets, known for piles of dung. With all the freight traffic through town, no one seemed to be able to find a solution for the mess the horses and mules left behind.

Few of the town's inhabitants wandered the streets at this hour. Most were at home for their evening meal or somewhere like Señora Arvizu's eatery. Quinn grimaced at the thought of spending the night at the jail. He couldn't leave a female occupant by herself all night even with the door locked. He'd have to set up a cot. Sleeping on an uncomfortable bed made the thrill of catching the Widow fade a little. Pushing away the thought, he resumed the walk toward the jail, thinking instead of the stir of excitement that would sweep the territories when he sent a telegram tomorrow announcing the capture of the Veiled Widow.

The jail door complained loudly as Quinn pushed it open a few minutes later. The Widow was rubbing at her cheeks when he glanced her way. Had she been crying? In the dim light, it was hard to tell. Quinn snorted softly as he set the plate of food down and went out to fetch a cup of cold water. Just like a woman to resort to tears to get someone to feel sorry for her. Well, he wasn't letting down his guard around this woman. If he did, who knew how many more people would end up robbed or killed before her criminal activities ceased?

"I brought you some supper." Quinn slipped the plate and cup through the appropriate slots in the bars. The woman eased off the bunk and took the meal from his hands.

"Thank you." She balanced the plate on the cot, lifted her veil a bit, and drained the contents of the cup.

Guilt washed over Quinn. He should have given her some water before he went to find supper. He would have treated his horse better than he treated this woman. Just because she was a criminal didn't make her any less human. He could almost hear the lecture his pa would give him about treating others fairly despite their outward appearance.

"I'll get you more water." He put his hand through the bars. She gave him the cup, then sank onto the cot and picked up the plate as he left. A minute later, he carried the full mug back to find her staring at the plate balanced on her knees. "Is something wrong?"

"I. . .um. No, nothing." She picked up the tortilla, unfolded it, and turned it over as if examining it for some reason. Cocking her head to one side, she turned her face to him. "I don't mean to be rude, but can you tell me what kind of food this is?"

Quinn chuckled. "I hadn't thought this might be your first time eating Mexican food. That circle of dough in your hand is a tortilla. The Mexicans use it like bread. They scoop up their food into the tortilla or use it to get food on the fork. The other food is beans with chilies and some meat with peppers and vegetables mixed together. The taste is good, but you might find the food a little spicier than what you're used to."

She nodded and took a tentative bite, lifting the veil with the back of her hand. Quinn caught a glimpse of her perfectly formed chin before she dropped the veil and began to chew.

"You might have an easier time eating if you were to take off that veil. Seems to me the thing must get in the way a lot."

"I'm fine." She must have decided she liked the food.

Other than taking the time to retrieve ⎯⎯⎯ held, she continued to eat with dainty bites. ⎯⎯ back to his desk and sat down, trying to ignore ⎯⎯ want to think about how vulnerable she looked a⎯⎯⎯⎯⎯ over her plate, her delicate hands trembling just eno⎯⎯ to notice. How could this woman appear so miserable when she was covered from head to toe in black? Instead of giving the image of an austere matron, she portrayed that of a vulnerable, needy lady in distress. No wonder so many men had fallen under her spell.

The Widow stood and crossed to the cell door. "I've finished. Thank you for the food and water."

Quinn retrieved the utensils, placing the cup on his desk. Snagging his hat from the rack by the door, he hesitated before walking out. "I need to return these to the eatery. Then I'll be making my rounds. The door will be locked so no one will bother you."

Jamming the hat on his head, Quinn slammed the door behind him. Why had he said that? Since when did he need to explain himself and his actions to some common criminal? He stalked down the street, stopping at Señora Arvizu's to drop off the plate and fork. His foul mood stayed with him as he went throughout the town, checking doors of businesses already closed and greeting those still on the streets. Quinn hurried to get to the jail before full dark set in, since he'd left without his lantern. What had this woman done to him? He'd never gone off with his thoughts so mixed up before.

"Deputy Kirby. Quinn." A man's voice called out to him. Quinn turned. A man in a cavalry uniform moved slowly down the street, a woman heavy with child on his arm.

"Conlon." Quinn felt himself relax somewhat at the sight of his good friends. "What are you and Glorianna doing out so late? Taking a walk?"

Even in the dimness of the evening, Glorianna Sullivan's

eyes flashed fire. "Quinn Kirby, did you or did you not arrest my cousin?"

"Now why would I arrest your cousin? I don't even know who your cousin is."

Glorianna Sullivan could be a formidable force to reckon with when she was angry. Right now she appeared to be furious.

Conlon gave Glorianna a grin, pulled her closer to his side, and patted the hand she'd wrapped around his arm. "Glory's cousin, Kathleen, was supposed to arrive on the stage. I got home from the new fort site a little late. By the time we got there, the stage had gone. Kathleen's trunk was waiting by the side of the street, but she wasn't there. We heard you arrested a woman who got off the stage, so we've been looking for you."

A feeling of impending doom settled heavy on Quinn's chest. "I arrested a known criminal who came in on the stage. I didn't ask her name."

"What did she look like?" Sparks flew from Glorianna's green eyes.

From the storm building in Glorianna, Quinn knew his description fit that of her cousin. He felt like squirming, wishing the dark would close in and he could hide. That forlorn woman sitting in the dingy jail cell was Kathleen O'Connor, not the Veiled Widow. How would he ever explain this?

three

Long hours in a swaying stagecoach, uncertain about her safety, had taken a toll on Kathleen. Though normally very optimistic, right now she was so weary, she couldn't think straight. Every muscle in her body cried out in agony from the constant shifting on the long ride to Tucson. Road dust covered every inch of her body. She felt as if she hadn't had a bath in weeks rather than days. In fact, she smelled almost as bad as the filthy mattress underneath her. Despair became her companion in this cell. The dirt walls, probably made of the adobe bricks Glorianna had written to her about, started to close in around her.

Kathleen pulled the small but stylish hat from her head, sticking the hatpin through the side to keep it safe. She felt naked without the veil, yet she didn't care anymore. What did it matter if people saw her face? Her mother's gasp of shock at the thought filled her mind. Mother had always been embarrassed at having a marked daughter. Although treated well enough at home, Kathleen had to hide behind the veil when she went out in public. Even then, her mother never stood close to her or sat with her at church as if by distancing herself, she could avoid the taunting and ridicule Kathleen received.

Curling in a ball, Kathleen sank onto her side on the cot. Her tired brain barely registered the scratches dug into the adobe bricks. Prisoners before her had carved their initials or little notches, perhaps to count the days spent in this dismal place. Her eyes drifted shut. She knew she should pray for strength, for comfort, for the will to live—but she couldn't.

❧

"Now, Glorianna, please calm down. If this is your cousin, I've taken good care of her. She even had supper from Señora Arvizu's." Quinn bit his tongue to keep the stupid thing from flapping any more. He'd rather be caught between a mother grizzly and her squalling cubs than to face an angry Glorianna.

The trio continued on down the darkening street. Lamplight shone through windows. They kept to the edge of the walkway to avoid any refuse that might have been thrown out. Quinn knew the cities back East had a system for getting rid of sewage that kept their streets from smelling and looking so awful, but Tucson still hadn't advanced that far. Only in the past year had the Apache uprisings been brought under control, paving the way for more people to immigrate to the Southwest.

Deep shadows covered the door of the jail. Metal clanked against metal as Quinn inserted the key into the lock. Beside him, Glorianna tapped her foot. Conlon's low chuckle made the heat rush to his face. The cavalry lieutenant must know his spunky wife was making Quinn nervous. A grating sound accompanied the turning of the key. The door swung open.

"If you'll wait here, I'll light the lamp so you don't trip in the dark." Quinn stepped through the door. Silence greeted him.

"Do you mean you left Kathleen in the dark?" Outrage echoed in Glorianna's voice.

"Now you don't know if this is your cousin for sure." Quinn tried to defend himself. "Just wait until you get a look at her. I'm telling you, she fits the description I got of the Veiled Widow."

Flame flared, causing Quinn to squint as he lit the lamp. He lowered the wick, then turned to beckon Glorianna and Conlon inside. Glancing at the cell, he thought at first his prisoner had escaped. Lifting the lantern high, he was at the door in two strides. The black lump on the bed proved to be the woman, curled in a tight ball, her face resting on one palm. If not for the soft cadence of her breathing, he wouldn't have known she was alive.

"Kathleen!" Glorianna grasped the bars with her hands, trying to tug them open. "Quinn, you open this cell right now. That's my cousin, Kathleen. She is not the criminal you're looking for."

Quinn hesitated. "Are you sure? I don't want to let you in there if you're not positive she's your cousin. I can roust her so you can be sure."

Glorianna swiveled around to face him. Her fisted hands dug into her hips. Quinn fought a smile at her feistiness.

"I'd suggest you let my wife in the cell." Humor crackled in Conlon's tone. "I don't know of a criminal anywhere who could stand up to her. Do you?"

Quinn couldn't help the chuckle as he reached over to shove a key into the lock. "I see your point, Conlon. Maybe I should caution Glorianna not to harm my prisoner."

The door creaked as it swung open, but the woman on the cot didn't stir. With her knees drawn up near her chin, she reminded Quinn of a little child. A powerful longing swept over him to sit down, pull her into his lap, and let her know everything would be all right. He mentally shook himself as he stepped aside for Glorianna. He couldn't afford to become soft, or every lawbreaker this side of the Mississippi would be heading this way for the easy pickings.

"Kathleen?" Glorianna started to kneel by the cot, then leaned over, instead. Quinn figured her condition hindered her movement. She brushed a hand across the woman's creamy cheek, getting no response. "What have you done to her? Did you knock her out so she wouldn't try to escape while you strolled around town at your leisure?"

"Now, Glory, you know Quinn wouldn't do such a thing." She sighed and sank down on the edge of the bed. "I know.

I'm sorry, Quinn. You're only doing your job. I've been as cantankerous as a grizzly bear lately."

Conlon chuckled, then sobered as she glared at him. "I imagine Kathleen is exhausted from the trip across the country. That's enough to wear anyone out."

Glorianna nodded as she continued to stroke Kathleen's forehead. "What should we do? We can't leave her here all night. We don't have the wagon for her to ride home in, either. When we found her bags, Pedro took them on home. I suggested to Conlon that we could walk to Señora Arvizu's to see if Kathleen was waiting there."

"Tell you what." Quinn hoped to get in Glorianna's good graces with his suggestion. "I noticed Doc Meyer's buggy tied up in front of the drugstore. Why don't I run down there and see if I can borrow it to take you home?"

A frown creased Glorianna's forehead. "Don't you let Doc Meyer drive us, though. That man goes faster than a hawk can dive. He's a danger to this town."

Conlon laughed. "He's never run over anyone. Besides, maybe he's trying to create a little business for himself."

By the time Quinn returned with the buggy, Glorianna informed him they'd decided to not wake her cousin since she appeared to be so exhausted. As Conlon helped his wife outside, Quinn picked up Kathleen. Amazement streaked through him at how light she was. How could he have made such a mistake? He gave a silent groan as he considered that he hadn't even asked her name or the identity of the person she planned to meet. What kind of lawman was he?

Turning sideways to ease past the bars, Quinn noticed the black hat and veil still resting on the cot. He paused, gazing down at the birthmark on her cheek. Some people would say it marred her beauty, but he knew differently. This was one special woman. The star-shaped mark proved that. He would leave the hat and veil here. Tomorrow, when she'd had a chance to recover some, he would show up at the Sullivans' home to apologize and return her belongings. Then he would have one more chance to see those gorgeous hazel eyes.

❧

The aroma of bacon frying tried to draw Kathleen out of her sleep. She fought waking, burying her face in the soft pillow, breathing in the freshness of newly washed laundry. Her eyes snapped open. A pillow? Clean, sweet-smelling sheets? Last night she'd fallen asleep in a grimy jail cell. Where was she?

She lay on a mattress on the floor of someone's parlor. A tall writing desk stood in one corner, the top open, with pen and paper ready for use. A small bookshelf stood nearby, holding several volumes. An oval braided rug covered most of the floor, the mix of colors testifying to someone using scraps of material from her sewing.

Kathleen sat up. A momentary wave of dizziness washed over her. She couldn't remember when she'd been so worn out. It was hard to even think. How had she come to be in this house? Surely that deputy wouldn't have allowed her to leave. . .and if he did, how did she get here when she didn't recall a thing?

A table near the doorway held a large pitcher and basin. A cloth for washing and a towel lay beside them. Kathleen stood on protesting legs and made her way over. Right now, washing up sounded like the biggest treat she could have. The cool water refreshed her, giving her a renewed desire to find out where she was. She turned to the bed, pulled the covers down, and searched for her veil. Her headgear was nowhere to be found. How could she go anywhere without it?

Soft footfalls sounded in the hallway outside the room. Panic shot through Kathleen. She gave the room a frantic glance, wondering where she could hide even when she knew hiding was futile. Whoever brought her to this place knew she was still here.

"You're awake." Glorianna's familiar voice brought Kathleen around. Tears of relief burned in Kathleen's eyes.

"Oh, Glory, it's so good to see you." Kathleen rushed into her cousin's embrace. She had no idea how she'd gotten to Glorianna's, but her heart sang a song of thanks to God. Had the jail and her arrest been only a bad dream? Somehow in the light of day, with her cousin's arms around her, it seemed that way.

"I thought you were going to sleep until Christmas." Glorianna's green eyes sparkled.

"What time is it?"

"Almost time to start some lunch for us. You'd better take time to eat a little breakfast first." Glorianna began to tug on her arm to pull her down the hall. "We can talk while you eat, then I'll see to getting you some bath water. I remember traveling out here and how much I wanted a bath."

"That sounds like heaven." Kathleen could feel the heaviness of yesterday fading. The smell of food made her mouth water and stomach growl. She waited to speak until she was seated at the table with Glorianna, a plate of food in front of her.

"I feel so disoriented. I remember falling asleep last night in a jail cell. Was that a bad dream? How did I ever get here without remembering anything?"

As Kathleen ate, Glorianna filled her in on the previous night's events and how their friend, Deputy Quinn Kirby, had mistaken her for a desperado. In the bright light of day, with a stomach full of food and the promise of a bath, Kathleen could finally see humor in the mistake.

"Tell me about the baby, Glory." Kathleen reached over to give a soft pat to Glorianna's rounded stomach. "When do you think the little one will arrive?"

"Not soon enough." Glorianna groaned and relaxed in the chair. "This one has to be a boy with six legs and eight arms. He kicks and pushes on me all the time. I had no idea babies could be so active before they were born. Who knows how I'll be able to keep up with him once he's here."

Kathleen laughed. "Sounds to me like you might be having a girl like you. I remember your mother making a few complaints about the trouble she had with you."

"Me?" Glorianna batted her eyes, then laughed. "I'd say that I hope the baby would be more like Conlon than me, but I've heard from his mother, and he wasn't an angel, either. I think we're doomed no matter what. This one will be the terror of Tucson."

"Speaking of Conlon, when will I get to meet this mysterious husband of yours?"

"He'll be home this evening. Every day he rides out to oversee the building of the new Fort Lowell. It's about six or seven miles from town. The first buildings are almost done."

"I thought you were living at the fort." Kathleen took a long drink of water to finish washing down her breakfast.

"We were." Glorianna sighed and shook her head. "Conlon decided I needed to be somewhere else. Because of the old fort's location, there's too much sickness. That's why the cavalry is building the new one outside of town." She leaned forward and rubbed her back. "It should have been done ages ago, but they have had so many delays for money, goods, and all. I can't wait to move there. Maybe in a few days Conlon can drive us to see what they've gotten done."

Kathleen frowned. "If the drive is that long, maybe we should wait until the baby comes."

Glorianna stood. "I don't know. Maybe the rough wagon trip will convince the baby to get here faster. Come on, I'll show you to your bath. I had Pedro draw the water for you."

A sigh of contentment escaped as Kathleen sank into the warm water. The tub was smaller than the one she used in her parents' home, but this one felt better. Her aching muscles protested every movement, and she hoped the warmth would loosen them. Glorianna left her with a bar of lavender-scented soap and instructions to be sure to take her time. She was to rest up for a few days anyway. Kathleen didn't argue. She had to smile at the changes she'd seen in Glorianna—the calmness and peace she didn't used to have. There was still the same bossy girl underneath, however, this time tempered with God's love.

After washing the grit from her hair, Kathleen frowned at the dingy water left in the tub. Who would have thought a person could get so dirty just from traveling? This water looked as if a bunch of hooligans had trekked through mud, then bathed.

Donning a fresh gown retrieved from her trunk before bathing, Kathleen felt almost presentable. She combed her long hair, twisting it up on her head in the latest fashion. The only things missing were her hat and veil. She didn't mind leaving her face uncovered around Glorianna, but she couldn't go out of the house without being concealed. Maybe Glorianna knew where it was. She'd have to ask.

Her shoes clacked noisily on the floor as she headed for the kitchen. Glorianna said she would probably be there working on lunch. At the time, Kathleen couldn't imagine eating anything else, but already her stomach seemed to have ideas of its own. She'd never had an appetite like this.

"Glory, have you seen my hat and veil? I can't find where I placed them last night." Seeing her cousin at work near the stove, Kathleen stepped through the kitchen door.

Glorianna turned, a smile lighting her face. "I believe you'll find them on the table."

Puzzled, Kathleen turned, wondering why she hadn't noticed they were there when she ate breakfast earlier. Deputy Quinn Kirby sat at the table, a grin on his face, her hat and veil dangling from his fingers. Kathleen slapped a hand to her cheek and wished the floor would open up and swallow her.

four

Turning her face to the side so her birthmark was away from the deputy, Kathleen held out her hand for her headgear. She couldn't imagine why Glorianna allowed this man in here. Then she remembered all the times Glorianna lectured her on not hiding her beauty behind that veil. Glorianna always thought Kathleen's mother had done her a disservice by convincing her she should conceal her shame.

From the corner of her eye, Kathleen could see the deputy grinning at her. Was he making fun? Did he think he could waltz in here after the fiasco yesterday and laugh at her? Anger swelled through her in a mighty wave.

"I believe you have something that belongs to me." She reached out to grab the items from him. "And I see no reason to laugh at someone for a deformity."

The infuriating man swept her hat and veil to the side, out of her reach. His grin faded to be replaced by a look of astonishment. A faint red flush colored his cheeks.

"I am not laughing at you, Miss O'Connor." He stumbled to his feet as if he'd just recalled his manners. "I had no intention of coming here to gloat at your expense." He moved closer. "Besides, I smiled in an effort to ease the way to an apology since I mistook you for a criminal yesterday. It was an honest mistake, but one I'm heartily sorry for."

Kathleen considered stepping away as he approached. After what he'd done to her yesterday, she had every reason to dislike him. Instead, she found herself drawn to him. *Most likely as a moth is drawn to a flame,* she chided silently.

He reached out and grabbed her hand, sending a shock

through her. "Here are your belongings. They were left at the jail." He still held her. She wanted to pull free, but couldn't seem to move.

"Furthermore, I can't stop you from hiding behind that silly thing, but I will say this: I think it's a fool thing to do. You have beautiful eyes and a beautiful face." He tugged her an inch closer, his eyes gray with emotion. "I don't know why you're ashamed of yourself, but I think it's too bad."

"I beg your pardon." Kathleen found the strength to try to free herself from his grasp. He held tight. "I am not ashamed of myself, and if I were, it would be none of your business."

"If you're not, then why do you hide behind that veil? You sure acted embarrassed yesterday when you lost it."

Kathleen tried to think of something to say. Was he right? Had her mother's shame become her own? For so long, she'd convinced herself she wore a covering to protect others. That had to be the reason.

"I know how people are horrified to see something like the mark I have. I'm simply saving them from embarrassment."

An emotion she couldn't identify swept across his face. Was it sympathy? Understanding? His expression softened, and a small smile lifted the corners of his mouth.

"I do understand. Perhaps more than you know." His grip loosened, and she pulled free, clasping her hands together to keep from shaking. He glanced down, then up into her eyes. "If I've offended you, I apologize. I still think you're hiding a lot of beauty. I'd appreciate your not wearing that contraption around me."

He slapped his hat onto his head and stepped toward the door. Nodding to Glorianna, who for once had been silent during the whole interchange, he opened the door. He looked at Kathleen and tipped his hat. "Remember what I said. I'd hate to mistake you for some criminal and have to arrest you again."

The door had barely closed behind him when Glorianna

burst into peals of laughter. She clutched her sides, gasping for air. Kathleen didn't know whether to join her cousin laughing or to stomp her foot in anger. She looked at the pathetic scrap of netting in her hand and decided merriment was much better than anger.

"I declare, Kathleen." Glorianna's face nearly matched her red hair. "I believe you two are meant for each other."

The laughter died in Kathleen's throat. "I can't believe you said that." Horrified, she stared at her cousin. "You know I can't be serious about any man—especially not one like that."

"I only know I haven't seen sparks fly like that since Conlon and I met." Glorianna grinned. "Besides, I know nothing of the sort about you not being able to get married. That was your mother's notion and a wrong one at that. My mother always encouraged you to consider marriage." Setting the pot on the stove to simmer, Glorianna crossed to the table, where a pile of sewing waited.

Sinking into a chair across from her cousin, Kathleen watched Glory's needle dip in and out of the white material. What looked to be a baby's nightgown rapidly took shape beneath her nimble fingers. Glancing at the pile of diapers waiting to be hemmed, Kathleen took up a needle, thread, and a diaper and joined Glorianna in her work. She needed time to think.

There had been a mistake here. She felt no attraction to the deputy. *The very handsome deputy with the compelling eyes*, she found herself thinking. The needle poked into her finger. She wiped the blood on a scrap of cloth before continuing.

How many times had her mother cautioned her to stay away from men? "You'll end up with a child just like you." Her mother would stand there lecturing, her hands on her hips, brow furrowed in a frown. "Imagine putting a child through the agony you've gone through? I don't see how you could ever want to do that."

Kathleen never summoned the courage to tell her mother that her life would have been bearable if she'd had some support at home. Instead, all she faced were more shame and ridicule. The only satisfaction she got was being in charge of her younger siblings. They loved her for who she was, not for how she looked.

Her aunt and Glorianna, on the other hand, always loved her and accepted her as a special child of God. The memory of the day the three of them sat sewing while mother was out came flooding back. She could clearly recall her aunt's gentle voice. "Kathleen, someday you will make some young man a wonderful wife. Don't deprive yourself of one of God's greatest gifts. Consider yourself as worthy as any other girl to marry and have children. God loves you so much. He wants the best for you."

Did God truly want her to marry? She understood God loved her as she was, but could someone else love her the same way? How could any man get past her outer ugliness?

૨૦

Flipping the reins over his horse's neck, Quinn swung into the saddle. He needed some time alone, and he'd promised Conlon he'd come out to the new Fort Lowell to see how the building was progressing. Ever since the contract came through for Lord and Williams to supply the adobe bricks for the buildings, Conlon had been hard pressed to have any free time. Quinn knew he chafed at leaving Glorianna for so long each day, especially with the fort so far from town. Having Kathleen here would be a relief for him.

Quinn tipped his hat to the mayor, John Allen, as he urged his horse to a faster pace near the edge of town. Being a deputy certainly had good points and bad ones. Keeping the peace and making sure people were safe gave him great satisfaction. Dealing with the officials could sometimes give him a headache, even if they were good men.

The sun shone bright, warming the crisp, clear day. Quinn's thoughts began to drift to the subject he wanted to avoid thinking about—his visit with a certain young lady this morning. A groan escaped as he thought of the stupid way he'd acted in front of Glorianna and Kathleen. When Kathleen entered the kitchen, he'd been so enamored, he'd forgotten his manners, sitting there with a coyote-that-caught-the-chicken grin on his face. His horse slowed to a walk, something the beast did whenever Quinn wasn't paying close attention. Quinn eased in the saddle and let him walk as he envisioned Kathleen bright-eyed and without her veil.

Her hair, still damp from washing, shone in the morning light. She wore it wrapped up in a very becoming fashion, but he wondered what she would look like with it hanging loose about her shoulders. He could still recall yesterday when she fell in the street and her hair loosened, allowing more than a few tendrils to come down. Even that wasn't like seeing it all flowing freely around her.

Quinn frowned. The only problem with the woman was her idea that people would dislike her because of the birthmark on her left cheek. His finger itched to trace the line of her intriguing star. He couldn't imagine how she'd gotten the idea that the birthmark detracted from her looks. She was a beauty who had been hidden for too long. He'd have to see what he could do about that.

The ride to the fort passed by too quickly. Quinn would have liked a little more time to get his thoughts in order before facing Conlon. He knew his friend wouldn't resist ribbing him for arresting Glorianna's cousin. Conlon didn't know, and Quinn hoped he wouldn't guess, that Quinn was the one most relieved that Kathleen wasn't a criminal. He'd hate to think he could have such an immediate attraction to someone who lived her life outside of the law. The most important measure in determining a person's worth should be their ability to live within the law.

"Hey, Quinn! Over here." Conlon waved from across the parade ground. Quinn waved, swung down, and watered his horse before tying him in the shade. The buzz of conversations from men at work droned in the air. Glancing around, he could see a lot of progress since his last visit to the site. The men had been working hard.

" 'Morning." He greeted Conlon with a slap on the back. "You sure accomplished a lot."

Conlon grinned. "I figure we need to work fast before the government decides on better ways to spend the money and takes the rest. Follow me and I'll show you where everything will be. By the time Glory and I move out here, we'll have our own doctor and hospital in case anything should happen. That's one of the worries Glory always had about being so far from town."

Quinn followed Conlon about the fort, admiring the buildings and the setup. "Has Glorianna been out here lately?"

A frown creased Conlon's brow. "She wants to come awful bad. I want her to wait until the baby arrives. She's getting so big, I figure the baby could come any time. I refuse to be between here and Tucson and have to deliver a baby."

Quinn laughed and clapped him on the shoulder. "I imagine you've delivered a colt or two. You should be able to handle one little baby."

Conlon chuckled. "The only way I know to deliver a baby is to rub the mother with straw to wipe the sweat off and rub her nose whispering things like, 'Good girl, you're doing fine.' Somehow, I don't think Glory would appreciate that."

They both laughed as they walked toward the parade ground. "I went by your house this morning to deliver some things Glorianna's cousin left at the jail. Your wife seemed pleased to have her cousin visiting."

"And how was Kathleen this morning? Since she was sleeping when I left, I still haven't met her." Conlon's intense blue eyes studied Quinn, making him want to squirm. Why had he mentioned Glorianna and Kathleen?

"She looked refreshed from the trip. I do believe she liked her accommodations at your house better than the ones at the jail. She didn't seem particularly happy to see me."

"She doesn't know you." Conlon strode across to the stable area. "Why don't you come to supper tonight? I'm sure Glory won't mind. She loves company. That way you can get to know Kathleen in a more relaxed atmosphere than the jail."

"Naw, you need the time to get to know her without me intruding."

"You aren't intruding. I invited you." Conlon slung a saddle on his horse and began to adjust the cinch. "If I didn't know better, I'd think you might be a little sweet on Miss O'Connor, Deputy."

"I only met her yesterday—and then I thought she was a criminal. How could I be sweet on a woman that fast?"

Conlon swung up on his horse. "Well, I knew the minute I met Glory that she was the one for me. I'd been praying for a wife, and when I saw her, I knew God brought her all this way just for me. Now, how about we head for town? I need to get Josiah Washington to do some shoeing for the cavalry."

Quinn tugged his horse's reins free and mounted. "Well, I haven't been praying for a wife. If and when I decide to get married, I don't need any help from anyone, God included."

Conlon's shoulders stiffened, and Quinn knew he'd hurt his friend again. He hadn't meant to. Conlon and Glorianna couldn't seem to understand why he didn't mind them believing in God and praying. If that worked for them, fine. They could worship however they wanted. Quinn's parents were Christians, but he knew he didn't need anyone bossing over him. He could manage his own life quite nicely. If he decided to pursue Kathleen, then that would be his choice—not something brought about by a God who lived in some far-off place watching over everyone. He had parents as a boy. Now, as a man, he answered to no one.

Nudging his horse, Quinn caught up with Conlon. "I didn't mean to offend. I'm glad your God brought you a wonderful wife, if that's what you believe. All I'm saying is, I'd like to pick out my own wife when the time comes."

"I understand, Quinn." The smile had faded from Conlon's face. "I used to feel the same way you do. I'll pray you turn your heart to God before it's too late."

The thunder of hooves interrupted them. A horse raced around a bend toward them. They rode ahead to meet the rider. Tugging the reins, the young boy almost lost his seating as the horse slid to a stop. Conlon reached out to grab the horse's bridle.

"Paulo, what's wrong?"

Quinn recognized the son of Pedro and Alicia Rodriquez, the couple who worked for Conlon and Glorianna. Paulo looked pale and ready to fall from the horse.

"The señora. She is having baby." Paulo looked frightened. "Doctor say to get you home."

Panic crossed Conlon's face. "Something must be wrong. Why else would they send for me?"

five

Swallowing a grin, Quinn urged his horse to catch up to Conlon's. He couldn't understand what possessed a normally rational, in-charge man like Conlon to fall apart at the mention of a woman having a baby. Glorianna was healthy and fit. Didn't women have babies all the time? Most of the families he knew had several children, and the wife was just fine. This wasn't the Dark Ages. Between the doctor and women with midwife experience helping Glorianna, this baby's birth should be easy.

The doctor shouldn't send for the father until the baby arrived. That would save hours of floor-walking distress for the husband. After all, what could he do at the house? Husbands weren't allowed to help with the delivery, although Quinn couldn't imagine why a husband would want to. The father always seemed to be in the way as the doctor's helpers hurried from one task to another. A father-to-be should be left at work, content in his ignorance, until the baby made an appearance.

The day had turned warm, and Quinn could see the sweat starting to lather up on Conlon's horse. Ridden like this, the animal would be overheated by the time they arrived in town.

"Conlon, slow down." Quinn urged his gelding to a faster pace and drew up alongside his friend. "Running your mount into the ground won't help Glorianna or the baby."

Blue eyes, glazed with worry, glanced his way. As if he suddenly realized what he was doing, Conlon pulled on the reins. Both horses slowed, their breaths huffing out in sharp pants. Patting his mount's neck, Conlon grimaced.

"Sorry. All I could think of was getting home to Glory. I

hate being so far from her when she needs me." Panic swept across his face again.

"She's got the doc looking after her. Don't worry." Quinn spoke in the soothing voice he used when calming a skittish mount or an angry drunk. "Besides, you know Alicia is there. She's had six kids of her own and probably delivered who knows how many others."

A shuddering sigh rippled through Conlon, making his shoulders quake. "I know you're right. I'm fine now." He rubbed a hand over his face. "I don't know why I can't trust God with everything the first time, but even now I run off trying to take care of everything myself." He grinned. "When will I learn? All I have to do is pray, and God will handle everything else."

Quinn groaned. Not another religion lesson. Conlon must have read his look, because he tipped his head back and laughed. How could the man be in a panic one minute and completely at peace the next? An uncomfortable reminder pricked Quinn's conscience. This was the same kind of peace his parents demonstrated when they went through difficulties. They would go off together, pray, then not be bothered by anything.

The steady thump of the horses' hooves in the dry dirt had a calming effect. Small waves of dust blew into the brush at the side of the road, coating the deep green leaves of the mesquite trees and creosote bushes with a layer of tan. Conlon appeared to be deep in thought, probably about his wife and child. Quinn began to relax.

Almost a mile passed with Conlon urging the horses on at a trot, fast enough to speed the trip home, slow enough to keep their mounts from overheating.

Conlon glanced over, his forehead furrowed. "Do you mind if I ask you a personal question, Quinn? One friend to another."

Quinn studied Conlon for a long moment, trepidation making him hesitate. "I guess I don't mind. That doesn't mean I'll answer." He cracked a grin. "If you're asking me what to name the baby, I'll have to tell you the only names I've ever given were to dogs and horses. How would Glorianna like a daughter named Brownie or a son named Buster?"

Conlon chuckled. "I'm glad I wasn't asking for help with names. I think Glory and I can manage that quite nicely." His grin faded. "I wanted to ask something about your growing up."

Quinn's horse snorted and pranced to the side as Quinn's legs tensed.

"You told me once before that your parents are as bad as me and Glory when it comes to talking about the Bible and the Lord. I don't want to be nosy, but I'm curious as to why you're so against anything Christian when your parents are firm believers."

The reins dug painful grooves into Quinn's palms. He and Conlon had grown pretty close in the last few months since the Sullivans moved to Tucson from Camp MacDowell. Their respective jobs brought them in close contact, and the friendship had developed from there. Conlon was easy to talk to. He often listened when others jumped to conclusions without considering the surrounding circumstances. Maybe if Conlon understood his reasons for turning away from God, he would leave him alone. After all, if Christians could go around explaining their faith to everyone, why couldn't he explain his beliefs, especially since Conlon asked?

"I used to think like you do." Quinn forced his hands to relax on the reins, and his horse settled into a steady walk. "I went to church every Sunday with my family. I joined them in prayer at mealtimes and even listened at night when my dad read to us from the Bible. I agreed with most everything they said until about a year before I left home."

The silence stretched as long-forgotten images flashed

through Quinn's mind. He could see his sister, Elizabeth, seated on the floor, a book in her lap. His mother would be in the rocking chair working on the never-ending pile of mending, while his dad's deep voice filled the house, sometimes sounding like what Quinn thought of as the voice of God Himself.

"What happened to change you?" Conlon appeared genuinely interested.

"A new family moved to town." Buried anger burned in Quinn's gut. "They had a boy a little older than me. Rupert Magee was the biggest bully I've ever met. He and his dad were large men, and both thought they should rule over everyone. Rupert took a dislike to my family for reasons I won't go into. He hated my sister, Elizabeth. At first he only yelled taunts at her in front of her friends. That hurt, but she and my folks prayed about it and said it would be all right. I wanted to pound Rupert into the ground."

Quinn's horse began to prance sideways down the road. "My dad tried talking to Rupert's dad, but Mr. Magee always defended his son. He said Elizabeth deserved what she got. Since they never did more than talk, there was nothing the law could do."

"I remember my mama saying words only hurt you if you let them." Conlon reined his horse around a gopher mound. "I think it's impossible for kids to ignore something said in cruelty. That kind of hurt is hard to heal. Did he ever do more than taunt her?"

Quinn's jaw tightened. "Not openly. Rupert took to following Elizabeth, but she didn't say anything for fear that I would get riled. Two days before I left, he followed her home from town and pelted her with rocks. We found out he'd done it before, but he'd never hit her. This time she came home with a knot on her head, the cut beside it bleeding all over. She also had a bruise on her back from a rock.

"I wanted to fight Rupert so bad, I could feel my fists hitting him. My pa stopped me, saying we needed to do this legally. We went to the sheriff. He was afraid of Rupert and his daddy. He wouldn't do a thing. Pa said that was God's answer."

"That would be enough to rile any boy," Conlon said.

"You're right. I was angry at my dad, angry at Rupert, and most of all, angry at God. All this time I believed God would protect His own, but now I knew different. I knew I couldn't stay around and believe in a God who made promises He didn't keep."

The clop of the horses' hooves and the jangle of their bits grated in the quiet. "Did you leave then?"

"I gave God one more night to do something. I thought maybe He was busy or Elizabeth wasn't important enough to take care of right away. Nothing happened, and I realized I had to handle things myself. When I had the chance, I packed a bedroll and loaded my horse. I didn't tell my folks I was leaving. I was so angry with them, I didn't think they deserved to know.

"That night I waited for Rupert at a spot I knew he'd pass by on the way home from a friend's house. I beat him almost senseless. After I had my revenge, I told him he'd better never even look at my sister again, or I'd hear about it and come looking for him. Then I climbed on my horse and haven't been home since."

Conlon's brows drew together. "So how do you know he listened to you?"

"Because he's a coward. Bullies are always that way when someone stands up to them. Besides, I did write to my folks. After I cooled down, I wrote and asked them about Rupert. They said he left town shortly after I did. He and his dad moved, and no one knew where they went."

The first houses on the outskirts of Tucson came into sight around a curve in the road. Quinn's horse settled to a quiet walk. "I suppose you'll say what I did was wrong, but I don't agree with you. I took care of my sister that night, and I've been taking care of myself ever since. I don't need a God like yours to interfere with my life."

Conlon flashed a cocky grin. "I know how patient God is. When you're tired of doing everything yourself, He'll be waiting." He urged his horse to a trot. "Now, let's go see if I'm a father."

Quinn noted the relief he felt at finally sharing his story. Conlon hadn't rejected him for what he'd said. In fact, he didn't appear surprised at all. As they tramped from the stable to the house, Quinn clapped his hand on Conlon's shoulder.

"Thank you for listening and not lecturing me."

Blue eyes twinkled as Conlon glanced at him. "Who am I to chide you on your attitude toward God? Lecturing won't help. Only prayer will work, and you can bet I'm doing plenty of that."

The door snapped shut behind them. Alicia stood over the stove, dipping water out of a pot, sweat beaded on her round face. She gave Conlon a tired smile as she turned to leave the room.

"Wait, Alicia. How's Glorianna?" The calm appeared to have left Conlon. Before he could ask more, Alicia disappeared through the doorway. Conlon pulled off his hat and glanced at Quinn. "I don't know if that's good or bad."

Biting back a laugh at the lost little boy look on Conlon's face, Quinn took his elbow and ushered him over to the table. "Why don't you sit down while I rustle up some coffee? I'm sure everything is just fine. Alicia was just a bit rushed."

Continuing his one-sided conversation, Quinn lifted the coffeepot from the stove. The weight told him there was enough of the brew for both of them. After finding the cups, he poured coffee that must have sat on the hot stove all day. It looked strong enough to eat the cups, but that might be just what Conlon needed.

"Here, drink this." He placed the brew on the table in front of the dazed father-to-be and sank into a chair across from him.

Conlon's fingers wrapped around the mug. He took a drink, choked, grimaced, and took another swig. A high, thin wail caused Conlon to jerk, sloshing coffee on the table. His eyes widened. He relaxed, then grinned.

Standing, he looked at Quinn as if wondering how he'd gotten there. "I think that might be my baby."

Setting his cup on the table, Quinn swallowed a mouthful of coffee. "That's either your baby or a cat that got its tail stepped on."

Conlon gave a nervous chuckle at Quinn's attempted humor. "Should I go see if Doc will let me in?"

"I think you'd better wait." Quinn heard the tap of light footsteps. Kathleen hurried into the kitchen, her dark hair in disarray, her dress rumpled and damp. The ever-present veil hung askew, though it still covered her face. Even so, Quinn had never seen a more charming sight. She grabbed a pile of snowy towels and started to rush out of the kitchen, acting as if she hadn't seen the men frozen in place, watching her.

"Kathleen," Quinn said.

She stopped, her back stiffening. Quinn realized then that she'd been so focused on her errand, she hadn't seen them. "Kathleen, I think Conlon would like to know how Glorianna and the baby are doing."

Without turning, Kathleen replied. "The doctor will be out soon to talk to you. Glory's doing great." Then she disappeared as fast as she'd come.

Time stood still as Quinn tried to imagine the agony his friend felt. Had something gone wrong with the birthing? The baby wasn't crying. He knew a thousand problems were racing through Conlon's mind right now, and he didn't know how to help him. There wasn't a thing he could do.

Conlon sank into the chair, curled his fingers around the

coffee cup, and bowed his head. Quinn knew he must be praying. He'd seen his parents this way many times. The tension in Conlon's shoulders slowly relaxed. His grip loosened. An air of peace seemed to wrap around him.

A baby's cry once again echoed through the house. Conlon's head snapped up. Tears sparkled in his eyes.

A few minutes later, the tap of footsteps, moving at a slower pace, sounded in the hallway. Kathleen, her veil straightened and hair fixed, came into the kitchen. She carried a bundle of blankets in each arm. Halting just inside the doorway, she turned to face Conlon. He rose from the table and stepped toward her.

Lifting the two small bundles, she spoke in an awed voice. "Conlon, this is your son." Her head dipped as if she were looking from one blanket to the other. "And this is your daughter." A note of delight crept into her voice. "You have twins."

six

Kathleen hummed a soft melody as she rocked Angelina, Glorianna and Conlon's baby girl. Andrew lay fast asleep in the cradle, his shock of black hair sticking out from beneath the blanket covering him. She brushed her fingers through Angelina's deep red curls. They were downy soft and wrapped tightly around Kathleen's fingers.

Blinking away tears, Kathleen lifted the baby and kissed her soft cheek, breathing in the soapy smell of the infant. She hadn't realized how much her heart ached to have a child of her own. Knowing that could never be made this a bittersweet experience. These babies were so precious.

Thinking of the day three weeks ago when the twins were born, Kathleen chuckled aloud. She would never forget the look on Conlon's face when she introduced him to his new son and daughter. Sheets had more color than his face did at that moment. She'd been afraid he would pass out from the shock.

She couldn't help feeling a flutter of anticipation when she remembered the surprised look on Quinn's face. He had stopped by every day the last three weeks on one pretext or another. He always waited to see her if she was busy elsewhere. Glorianna did her best to leave the two of them alone despite Kathleen telling her not to. Glory said Quinn was sweet on her, but that didn't matter. She could never marry and preferred not to be tempted.

Tipping her head back against the rocker, Kathleen closed her eyes. Immediately, the image of blue-gray eyes, twinkling with humor, flashed across her vision. She had to do something to get Quinn interested in someone else. If he kept coming by, she wouldn't be able to deny the attraction between them.

The soft whisper of footsteps alerted her that company had entered the room. She opened her eyes to find Glory bending over the cradle. She sat up and Glory straightened.

"Who is the one needing the nap? You told me you were taking the babies to put them down, and here I find you taking a siesta." Glorianna grinned and reached for Angelina.

"I wasn't sleeping, just resting my eyes and thinking." Kathleen tried to sound miffed, then giggled.

"I think we're all a little tired. Who would believe something so small could make enough noise that would wake the entire household." Glorianna settled her daughter into the cradle beside her brother, rocking the tiny bed to ease their restlessness. "Conlon's men have been teasing him about the circles under his eyes, and he isn't even the one getting up in the night. I'm so glad you're here to help."

"I've been meaning to talk to you about that." Kathleen followed Glorianna to the kitchen, where they poured coffee and sat at the table. "You have such a small house. I thought maybe I should plan to leave so you could have the place to yourselves." At Glorianna's panicked look, she continued. "I won't do it right away. In a couple of weeks you'll have your routine down."

Glorianna's fingertips whitened on her coffee cup. "I'm so sorry you have to stay in the parlor. I know it isn't very private or comfortable. Our quarters at the new fort will be much better, but I don't know how soon we'll be able to move in." Her eyes glittered with tears. "Oh, Kathleen, I've enjoyed having you here. I can't bear the thought of you leaving. The trip east is so long. I thought you would stay through the winter."

"Glory, I didn't mean to leave the city. I want to stay. I love it here." Kathleen reached across the table and twined her fingers with her cousin's.

"I've heard that Mrs. Monroy, down the street, is letting rooms to young ladies. I thought I would talk to her about one. Her house is so close, I could walk over every day to visit and help out with the babies."

"But how will you afford to stay there?" Glorianna's shoulders relaxed as she took a sip of her coffee.

Excitement made it hard for Kathleen to sit still. "I've been thinking about that. The wives here aren't able to keep up with the eastern fashions. I've just come from there, and I'm an excellent seamstress. I thought I could offer my services to sew the latest in clothing for the ladies and men in Tucson. I brought the latest E. Butterick and Company's catalog with me. As the fashions change, I can have Mama send me the new catalogs showing the various styles. I can order material through the mercantile."

Kathleen forced herself to sit still and wait for Glory's opinion. Now that she was out from under her mother's oppressive guardianship, she wanted to stay here. The freedom she'd always longed for seemed attainable. Only one question remained unanswered. Could people accept her despite her birthmark? Would they consider her an equal or someone cursed, as her classmates once taunted?

"Would Mrs. Monroy let you run a business like this from her house?"

"I don't know. I need to ask. It would mean entertaining ladies in the parlor and in my room." Kathleen tried to control her eagerness, but knew she wasn't doing a good job. "Once I get started, I could look for a small building to let and have a little shop."

Glorianna frowned. A lump formed in Kathleen's throat. Did her cousin disapprove of her idea? Would she have the courage to continue with her venture if Glory didn't agree?

A smile lit Glorianna's face. "I think this is a wonderful idea. You'll have to adjust some of the patterns for the Southwest.

The heat in the summer makes the tight dresses unbearable. You'll have to learn about using lighter fabrics too."

"That won't be hard at all. I know a lot about different materials already. You can help me, and I'm sure the other ladies here will help out as well. Do you think. . . ?" Kathleen stopped, afraid to voice the question that scared her the most.

"Do I think what?" Glorianna's smile vanished.

Kathleen's hands twisted in her lap. She couldn't look at her cousin. The question burned inside, yet she feared to say anything.

"Kathleen, what is it?" Glorianna retrieved the coffeepot and filled their cups, giving Kathleen a few moments to compose her question.

Waiting for Glory to sit down again, Kathleen took a quick sip, scalding her tongue. She drew in a deep breath and faced her impatient cousin. Glorianna's foot tapped a rapid rhythm on the floor.

"I wondered if you thought people would be able to accept me."

"Accept you? What do you mean?" Glorianna leaned forward, eyes narrowed, looking as if sparks would soon fly. "Are you referring to the way you were treated in school?"

Kathleen nodded.

"I can't believe you even considered people out here might reject you because of a little birthmark. I don't know why you insist on wearing that ugly veil. The only reason I can think of is your mother's negative influence."

Glorianna moved to a chair beside Kathleen. She pulled Kathleen's hands into her lap and held them. "Listen to me. You are a beautiful person. You are not cursed. You know God loves you." Her grip tightened, becoming almost painful. "Trust me in this. No one will reject you because of your birthmark. God made you special. Don't be ashamed."

Kathleen glanced up, blinking rapidly. Glorianna caught

Kathleen's gaze. She grinned. "Besides, you know you have one admirer in town, and he's seen you at least twice without your veil. You haven't scared him off yet."

A sharp knock rattled the kitchen door. Kathleen tugged at her hands, but Glorianna wouldn't let go.

"Come on in, Quinn." Hidden laughter gave Glorianna's voice a musical lilt. The door opened. Kathleen heard the deputy sheriff's heavy footsteps. She tried to focus on her coffee cup on the table, but the pull of his gaze drew her eyes upward. When their eyes met, the connection was instant and powerful. Kathleen could feel the flush staining her cheeks.

"Good morning, Kathleen." Quinn smiled, twisting his hat in his hands. For some reason, she knew he wasn't at all uncomfortable seeing her without her veil. Even so, she would have covered her cheek with a hand if Glorianna hadn't held them both tight.

"Good morning, Deputy. Could I get you a cup of coffee?" Kathleen knew if he said yes, Glorianna would have to let her go. She could pour a quick cup, then dash to the parlor and retrieve her veil.

Still holding Kathleen's hands, Glorianna stood and offered her chair. "Here, Quinn, have a seat. I'll pour your coffee, then check the babies."

Kathleen gritted her teeth in anger. Glory knew exactly what she'd planned and had managed to keep her from escaping. Quinn settled in next to her.

"Did you know Kathleen is thinking of leaving us?" The sweetness in Glorianna's tone let Kathleen know her cousin was up to something. Quinn's eyes widened as he looked from Glorianna to Kathleen.

"Are you going back East so soon? Traveling so far in the winter months can be hazardous." A note of panic matched the look on his face.

"Oh, she's not leaving Tucson; she's only leaving our

house." Glorianna handed Quinn his coffee. "She wants to rent a room from Mrs. Monroy and open a dressmaking shop. If you're not too busy, maybe you could escort her to see about it."

Taking a long swig of coffee, Quinn studied her. Kathleen wanted to squirm.

"I have nothing pressing to do right now. If you're ready, I'll walk down the street with you. I'm sure the ladies in town would welcome a seamstress who is familiar with eastern fashions." He downed the rest of his coffee. "Shall we go?"

Standing, Quinn slapped his hat on his head and offered Kathleen his hand. She felt trapped. Part of her wanted to place her hand in his and walk out the door without a care; the other part feared the reaction of others on the street and wanted to hide.

"I have to get my hat and veil before I can go."

"The hat, I can understand. Ladies always want to wear a hat when they go out." Quinn frowned. "The veil you don't need." He started to touch her cheek, and she jerked away. "You have nothing to hide." His eyes were warm and compassionate.

"I'll get your hat." Glorianna hummed a light melody as she swept from the kitchen, returning momentarily with Kathleen's hat minus the veil. "Here you are. You tell Mrs. Monroy hello for me."

Before she knew what happened, the kitchen door banged shut behind them and Kathleen was standing barefaced beside Quinn in the bright fall sunlight. She stepped away, ready to turn and rush into the house. As if he sensed her fear, Quinn placed her trembling hand on his arm and smiled at her as if he hadn't a care in the world.

"I can't do this." Kathleen backed against the door. "I'm sorry. It has nothing to do with you. I'm just not ready yet." With a sad smile, Quinn opened the door and waited while she retrieved her veil.

On the short walk down the street, Quinn waved to the occasional rider or wagon passing by on the road. He kept her close to his side as if trying to reassure her that she would be fine. Kathleen began to relax.

"I'm guessing the kids you grew up around used to tease you about your birthmark."

Kathleen jerked at Quinn's blunt statement. No one had ever dared speak so openly to her.

"I used to know someone with a mark similar to yours. She got called names, accused of being cursed or of the devil. She was the sweetest girl. None of those accusations were true for her, and they aren't true for you." His serious gaze held hers.

"Maybe the person you knew didn't deserve the accusations, but I'm not that person. Please don't judge me by the same standard." Kathleen pulled her hand free. "Here is Mrs. Monroy's house. I believe you have other duties, Deputy Kirby. I can see myself home." She turned up the walkway to the large adobe house, hoping he couldn't see the regret eating a hole in her heart. No matter how painful she found it, she had to discourage him. This couldn't continue. She'd heard Conlon talking to Glorianna about Quinn's lack of faith. Even if she were free to marry, she could never wed someone who didn't share her love of the Father.

"You won't get rid of me that easily, Miss O'Connor."

She held her stance rigid as she knocked on the door, waiting for Mrs. Monroy to let her in. She refused to give Quinn the satisfaction of knowing how much she wanted to see if he was still there.

Lydia Monroy, a large woman with plump cheeks and kind eyes, exuded a warmth Kathleen found comforting. Chattering away, Lydia told of being a widow for three months and how she decided to take in boarders because her large home was lonely. She and her husband had never had children. All her family lived in the East. She wanted company to talk to during the long evenings.

"Breakfast and supper will be provided. When you move in, I'll let you know the schedule. We'll all sit down and eat at the same time." Lydia smoothed her hair and frowned. "I have two boarders arriving next week. Both new school-teachers will be staying here. With three unattached young ladies in the house, I'll have to make rules about gentlemen callers. I'll expect you to abide by them."

"That won't be a problem. I don't expect to have any callers." Kathleen looked around the airy room they'd entered.

"These will be your sleeping quarters." Lydia gestured around. "Now, you mentioned being a seamstress." She stepped to a door and opened it. "This room hasn't been used for years. If you're willing to help clean it up, you can use it for a shop. There is an outside door, so patrons can come and go without disturbing the rest of the house."

Kathleen peered into the dusty room. Cobwebs and layers of dust covered various items piled in the room. This would be perfect. She clasped her hands together to still the shaking.

"I'm sure we'll be able to come to terms." Lydia smiled at her. "I can't wait to be your first customer."

Kathleen was almost singing as she said good-bye to Lydia Monroy. They agreed she would come by every day to work on the room and could move in at the end of two weeks. She wanted to wait at least that long to continue helping Glorianna.

"You're looking pretty cheerful."

Kathleen clapped a hand to her mouth to stifle a shriek. Quinn lounged against a tree at the edge of the road.

"What are you doing here?"

"I told you, I'm not easy to get rid of." His lazy smile warmed her in a way she'd never felt before. He took hold of her hand and wrapped it around his arm, starting down the street toward Glorianna's house. "I'm afraid you may as well plan on seeing me around a lot. I've decided someone needs to introduce you to everyone in town so you can get used to us all. As a deputy, I know just about everyone." He grinned, and she couldn't remember why she hadn't wanted to be with him.

seven

Waiting for the stage's arrival, Quinn couldn't seem to keep his mind on his duty and off of Kathleen. Yesterday, she had moved into her new quarters at Mrs. Monroy's boardinghouse. For the past two weeks she had been hard at work helping Glorianna with the babies. Then, when they were napping, she would slip away and go to work on the room that would become her seamstress shop. He couldn't believe how she'd taken a dingy, cobweb-infested place and made it into an airy, inviting room. Yellow curtains draped across clean windows. Sunlight-brightened walls held swatches of colorful materials.

Although Kathleen continued to discourage his visits, Quinn couldn't make himself stay away. He'd never wanted to be tied down with a wife and kids, but for some reason, since he'd met Kathleen, that didn't matter so much. She still didn't feel comfortable going into town without her hat and veil firmly in place. He accused her of hiding her beauty from the world when, in reality, he only wanted to be able to see her himself. He didn't care if any of the other men in town could see her. There were so few single women here that those who came were pursued by so many men they often had trouble choosing one to marry. He didn't want that to happen with Kathleen. She should be for him alone.

A cloud of dust roiling in the air heralded the arrival of the stage. Quinn checked his pistol, lifting it, then dropping the gun into the holster. His badge shone. Although he didn't move other than to check his gun, his whole body tensed with readiness. Maybe today the Widow would be arriving on the stage. He still waited for her every day, hoping to catch her before she had the chance to harm one of the citizens under his protection.

The driver eased down off the coach, nodding at Quinn. After placing the small step stool on the ground, he opened the door and reached up to help someone down. Quinn tensed. His hand flexed above the handle of his pistol. A foot encased in a brown boot reached for the step. A woman in a gray dress, her hair upswept and topped with a matching gray hat, stepped down from the stage. She gave the driver a tired smile and moved away before turning around, as if waiting for someone else.

Some of the tension eased out of Quinn. He wondered who the new arrival was and if her husband accompanied her. Once more the driver reached up to help someone from the stage. This time a slender foot extended encased in black. Excitement coursed through Quinn. He gripped the butt of his gun. The woman who stepped down was garbed in black with a hat, but no veil. Dark hair, grayed by the road dust, was drawn up into a high, loose bun. Even from here, he could see a set of lively dark eyes taking in the town. She nodded to the driver and moved to stand beside the first woman. The two waited for bags from the top of the stage.

Neither of these two women was the Widow. Quinn sighed and dug his toe into the dry road. Why didn't she just show up? He was ready and waiting. The Veiled Widow wouldn't get past him. He'd been taking care of himself for years and had been a lawman in various cities for the past six years. His hunches always seemed to pay off. . .and right now, those hunches told him she would show up here in Tucson. When she did, he would be ready.

The huffing of a person in a hurry sounded from behind him. Quinn glanced around to find John Allen approaching at a faster pace than the man generally moved. His partially balding pate glistened with sweat as he removed his hat. He wiped his head with a handkerchief and slapped the hat back on.

"Afternoon, Mayor."

"Afternoon, Deputy. Sure is a warm one for November."

"Might be best to slow down." Quinn grinned. He rarely saw the mayor in such a hurry. "You act like you're heading for a fire."

Mayor Allen wiped a drip of sweat that ran down his nose. "I almost missed the stage. Have they arrived?"

"Who?" Quinn followed the mayor's gaze to the two women now standing next to a pile of trunks and bags at the side of the street. "Are those ladies relatives of yours?"

"What? Who?" Mayor Allen scrubbed at his mouth, looking flustered. "No, they're not. I'm here to meet them in an official capacity. These are the new schoolteachers the town hired. I sent for a boy to bring round a wagon to take them to their rooms. They'll be staying at Mrs. Monroy's boardinghouse."

Mayor Allen tore his gaze away from the two young women and glanced up at Quinn. A bright flush crept up his cheeks. "I can see we'll have a number of men interested in meeting these ladies."

Quinn chuckled and straightened from the wall. "Don't count me among them. I'd better be off on my rounds. Good day."

Striding down the street in the opposite direction of the jail, Quinn couldn't help wondering how Kathleen would take to the new arrivals. Would she hide her face from them too? A couple of times, he'd caught her working on the room without the veil, but she still wore the contraption around the house. Quinn gritted his teeth as a wave of anger swept through him. What he wouldn't give to have the chance to trounce the kids who'd taunted Kathleen when she was young. Whoever did this to her had done a thorough job. Parting her from her veil would be a major undertaking—one he considered a challenge.

A half-hour later, the low rumble of his stomach alerted

Quinn that evening had crept up on him. Turning in the direction of Señora Arvizu's eatery, he quickened his pace. When he arrived, several tables were already taken. The buzz of conversation carried a hint of excitement.

"Quinn, join us." Ed Fish waved an arm in the air. Quinn threaded his way through the crowd to the table occupied by Ed and John Wasson, owner of the *Citizen* newspaper.

"Evening." Quinn sank into a chair next to Ed and signaled to Señora Arvizu. She would bring his usual. "What's all the excitement?" Ed and John looked at him as if he'd grown an extra head.

"Haven't you heard?" Astonishment crossed Ed's face. "The new schoolteachers are here. We've seen them. I went with John to ask about interviewing them for the *Citizen*."

Quinn's lips twitched. "I didn't know you did articles for the paper, Ed."

Ed flushed. "I don't. John asked me to go along and meet the teachers. As a business owner, I wanted to make them feel welcome."

"It didn't hurt to see that they were pretty, either." John chuckled at his friend's obvious discomfort. "We didn't actually get the interview today. They were just moving in, but we did set up an appointment to talk with them tomorrow."

"I can't wait to read the article." Quinn picked up a fork as the señora placed a plate loaded with steaming food in front of him. "Did you happen to meet Glorianna Sullivan's cousin while you were there?" He tried to sound casual, hoping his friends wouldn't suspect where his interests lie.

Ed pushed his empty plate away. "Is she the one who always wears the veil?" At Quinn's nod, his brow furrowed. "I can't figure out why she does that. Any ideas?"

Shoveling a forkful of beans into his mouth, Quinn hoped to avoid the question. He'd brought this on himself by inquiring, but now he didn't want to answer. He shrugged.

"I haven't seen her," John said. "I've heard talk, though. Most people think she's a little standoffish. Maybe she's so ugly, she doesn't want anyone to see what she looks like."

Quinn choked. Ed pounded him on the back. Quinn took a deep breath, then a long swig of coffee.

"Have to be careful with that hot chili." Ed spoke with the conviction of one who knew. "I breathed in one of those chilies last week and thought I was gonna die." John nodded his agreement.

Pushing his plate to one side, Quinn stood. "I better be off again. 'Bout time to start my evening rounds."

"Hey, you goin' to the fandango next week?" John asked.

Quinn shrugged again.

"I'm going." Ed grinned. "I imagine every bachelor around will be there. Those new schoolteachers will have their feet worn off by the end of the night. I plan to try to get in my share of dances."

John rubbed his chin. "You know, Ed, I imagine those ladies will step around the floor more with the men they already know. What do you say to wandering over to the boardinghouse and getting better acquainted?"

Ed stood so fast he knocked over the bench he and Quinn had been seated on. His face reddened, and with Quinn's help, he straightened the bench. The three walked out into the fading light together.

"Why don't you come along with us, Quinn? Maybe one of these ladies will take a shine to you." Ed clapped him on the shoulder.

"Nope, I've got work to do. You boys go on ahead. Besides, if I were to show up, you two wouldn't have a chance with the ladies." They all laughed as they headed off in opposite directions.

The urge for Quinn to go by and see Kathleen was tempered by the knowledge that Ed and John would be there visiting the

new schoolteachers. Quinn didn't want them to realize his
interest lie in the mystery woman, not in the two unattached
teachers who had just come to town. Tomorrow morning, he
would go by and see how her shop opening had gone. He'd
check to see if she'd gotten any sewing assignments and, if
not, he would try to spread the word. Then again, Mrs. Monroy
would be her best customer for awhile, and she knew everyone
in town. News would get around.

❧

Kathleen's muscles ached from sitting so rigidly. For the last
hour, she'd been trapped in the parlor. She'd been visiting
with Mrs. Monroy and the two new schoolteachers, Maria
Wakefield and Harriet Bolton, when the callers began to
arrive. First, two of the town's prominent men came: John,
the owner of the paper, and Ed, who owned the flour mill.
She couldn't remember their last names.

A knock rattled the front door. Mrs. Monroy left the room.

Ed stood, his hat in his hands. "It's sure been a pleasure,
meeting you ladies. We'd best be on our way."

John jumped up. He followed Ed in lifting Maria's hand to
his lips for a quick kiss. He turned to Harriet, lingering a little over her fingers. Kathleen nearly groaned aloud at his
obvious infatuation with a woman he'd only known for an
hour. Maria and Harriet stood to walk their admirers to the
door, chatting easily. Kathleen relaxed her tense muscles and
prepared to escape to her room. Confusion reigned in the
hallway, keeping her inside the parlor until it was too late.

"Here you go, gentlemen." Mrs. Monroy gestured to the
two chairs recently vacated by Ed and John. Maria and
Harriet slipped into the room and resumed their seats.

"Kathleen, these are Thomas McKaye and Robert Beldon.
They've come by to meet the new ladies in town." Mrs.
Monroy beamed as if having all these men stop by had been
her idea.

Thomas, a tall, lanky man with a droopy mustache, nodded his greeting. Robert, as short and rotund as Thomas was tall, gave a grin that showed all eight of his teeth. They seemed to be waiting for Kathleen to say something. She opened her mouth, but nothing came out. Just as with Ed and John, she could think of nothing to say. She'd never had experience with small talk like this. Her mind went blank.

"Are you ladies planning to go to the fandango?" Robert gave another grin.

Maria smiled. "The last two gentlemen mentioned a fandango, but I'm afraid we easterners have no idea what you're talking about."

Thomas tapped the toe of his boot on the floor. He twisted his long mustache with a finger and thumb, giving himself a lopsided look. "Why, a fandango is just a dance. The Mexicans here are fond of having them. All the soldiers like to attend and we want as many of the single gals as we can get. There's usually quite a crowd."

"If you ladies would like, we could escort you to the dance." Robert looked hopeful as he stared at Maria and Harriet and pointedly ignored Kathleen.

Maria and Harriet exchanged glances. "I believe we'll be attending with Mrs. Monroy. Perhaps we'll see you gentlemen there," Harriet said.

The conversation continued as Kathleen sat still as a stone. She hoped no one would remember her presence if she didn't move or speak. Sitting in a parlor with men was a nightmare. She could only imagine how much worse attending a dance would be. *Please, help me find a way to stay home from this, Lord. You know how Glorianna likes to socialize. She'll expect me to go with her. I simply can't do that.*

She closed her eyes and pictured the horror of trying to learn dance steps that everyone else was good at, when she'd never done such a thing in her life. Other people didn't realize how hard a simple thing like walking was when you were wearing a veil. Of course, Glory's answer would be to leave the veil at home. How could she? Didn't Glorianna know how everyone stared at her with the veil? How much worse would it be when they could see the ugly mark disfiguring her cheek?

Before the next round of visitors could intrude, Kathleen escaped to her room. She stood in the dark, relief making her tired. A soft, rattling sound came from the room next door. Her heart began to pound. Someone was coming into her dress shop. Picking up a candlestick in one hand and a lamp in the other, she crept toward the door separating her room from her shop.

The figure of a man stood outlined against the window. As she moved the lamp to shine through the door, the gleam of a badge caught her eye.

"What are you doing here?" She hissed the words at Quinn, hoping everyone in the parlor wouldn't hear.

"I'm supposed to check on businesses and see that they're locked up for the night. I'm just doing my job." Quinn didn't look as certain as he sounded.

"You could get me kicked out if Mrs. Monroy caught you sneaking in here."

"I'm not sneaking; I'm checking."

"Well, everything's fine, so leave before you get caught."

Quinn's thumb rubbed across his badge, and he grinned. "I'll leave just as soon as you promise to go to the fandango with me. It's next week."

"I know when it is." Kathleen's voice began to rise above a whisper, and she glanced over her shoulder. "I can't go to a dance. I've never done such a thing, and I don't intend to start now."

"Have you ever heard me sing?" Quinn's question caught her off guard. He opened his mouth.

"Don't you dare. My reputation will be ruined. Now, leave quietly."

He grinned. "Just give me your word." She remained silent. "Okay, here's my favorite cowpoke song. I learned it not long after I left home." He opened his mouth again.

"No." Kathleen's teeth clicked together over the word. "All right, I'll go. But this is blackmail, and I believe it's illegal, Mr. Deputy Sheriff."

He chuckled and tipped his hat as he backed out the door. "I guess you'll have to tell the sheriff the whole story or arrest me yourself."

eight

"Glory, I can't do this." Kathleen tugged at her skirt, straightening it again. The green taffeta dress was the latest fashion. Beside her on the writing desk lay a matching green hat complete with a dark green veil.

Glorianna picked it up, stretched, and pinned the stylish hat in place. "You will be just fine, Kathleen. You've never seen anything like this fandango. The music is different. The dancing is fast and fun. Relax and enjoy the evening."

"But I told you what Quinn did. He blackmailed me into going. I can't go with him."

Glorianna placed her hands on her hips. "Why can't you go with him? The man is crazy about you. He asks Conlon questions every day."

"He doesn't believe in Jesus Christ, Glory. You know what the Bible says about being yoked to unbelievers. We're not to do that. Besides, someone like me can't marry."

"Aha." Glorianna crossed her arms and tapped her foot on the floor. "Now the truth is coming out. Are you still listening to what your mother told you about never having children?"

Kathleen could feel the heat in her cheeks. She bit her lip, trying to think of a quick answer that would satisfy her cousin and still not be a lie.

"I thought so." Glorianna took a step closer. "Now you listen to me. I know you remember my mother talking to you about your cheek. There is no reason for you to be ashamed."

Her tone softened, and Glory placed her fingertips over Kathleen's mark. "My mother told you this is as if God took a star from heaven and touched it to your cheek before you were

63

born. I always loved that thought. In fact, for a long time, I was jealous that God never did anything so special for me."

Tears glistened in her cousin's eyes, and Kathleen swallowed hard around the lump in her throat. She could still remember the day her aunt made that comment. She'd treasured the thought for years, even though she knew the rest of the world didn't view her deformity the same way.

"Kathleen, you were denied the fun most young women experience. You've let your mother's fears become your own. Give the people here a chance to know you. They aren't the children you grew up with."

"But I can't go with Quinn." Kathleen's voice sounded gritty from emotion.

"He's not asking you to marry him. You need to get out and meet the townspeople. Quinn knows everyone. He'll make sure you're introduced around." Glory smiled and stepped away. She tapped a finger on her lower lip. Kathleen wanted to cringe under the scrutiny of a cousin who knew her too well.

"Are you afraid of your feelings for him?"

Cold fingers of dread wormed their way through Kathleen. Did she have feelings for Quinn? She knew without thinking that her answer had to be yes. Over the last few weeks, she'd come to look forward to having him around. He had seen what she looked like and never made fun or acted as if she was different from any other woman on the street. When he stopped in at the boardinghouse, he was polite to Maria and Harriet but paid special attention to her. For the first time in her life, Kathleen was being courted by a man—one she found thoroughly attractive, no less. Somehow she had to deny these feelings before they carried too far. There were too many reasons she couldn't have a relationship with the handsome deputy.

A faint knock sounded from the front door. They heard the

thump of booted feet as Conlon strode down the hallway to answer. Kathleen had told Quinn she would be at Glorianna's getting ready. Conlon and Glorianna were going to the fandango too. Glory insisted the babies would be fine. Usually, the older women loved to care for the babies while their mothers danced. This would be the first time they'd get to watch Glory's twins, and Kathleen had heard there were several ladies vying to be the first to hold them.

"Kathleen, Quinn's here." Conlon stuck his head in the room, his black hair in total disarray, his clothes unchanged. He grinned at Glory's look of dismay. "I'm a fast dresser. I'll be ready before Angelina cries." They heard him rush down the hall to the bedroom.

"When he grins at me that way, I wonder how his mother could ever punish him." Glorianna sighed. "I can almost see the cute little boy he was. I'm hoping Andrew doesn't ever grin at me like that, or he'll get away with anything."

Tamping down her nervousness, Kathleen gave a strangled sound she hoped passed for a laugh. "You always were one to let the boys' smiles get to you." She glanced at the door. Her fingers twined together, squeezing until she wondered if the bones would crack. *Jesus, help me. I have to find a way to discourage Quinn. . . . And he's the most persistent man I've ever known.*

A faint wail sounded from Glorianna's bedroom. "That sounds like Angelina. I guess that means Conlon is ready to go." Glorianna chuckled and swept from the room to retrieve her unhappy child.

Kathleen watched her cousin leave. Quinn was waiting in the sitting room. She should be happy to be going to the fandango with such a handsome man. Why, all the girls there would probably want to dance with him. Kathleen gasped. That was the answer to her problem. Relief swept through her. Her fingers unclenched, and she touched her hat to make sure it was firmly pinned in place. Straightening her shoulders, she marched out the door and down the hallway to meet Quinn.

❧

Quinn stared out into the darkness, the lamp behind him giving an eerie reflection in the glass. A leather vest stretched taut across his chest, his only concession to the cool November evening. Cold rarely bothered him. Here in Tucson the weather didn't get chilly enough to worry about. When he'd worked up in the northern territories, the cold had been fierce enough to make a man want to hibernate right along with the bears.

A gleam caught his eye. He'd wondered about leaving his badge and gun at home but thought better of it. He never knew when conflict could break out at one of these dances. Usually, it wasn't anything too big. Some fella would get jealous of another, probably because of a pretty señorita they both wanted to dance with. Quinn grinned to himself and rocked back on his heels. He had the advantage over all the other men in town. He knew where the prettiest girl lived, and they had no idea. Maybe tonight Kathleen would leave her veil at home. Being seen at the fandango with her on his arm would give Quinn no end of pleasure. All the unmarried men in town would burn with jealousy.

More and more, he heard speculation about why Kathleen wore a veil all of the time. Although he hadn't said anything, Quinn had been chuckling to himself, wondering what these men would say if they knew the truth. Meanwhile, every day he made some excuse to visit her. A few times lately, she had even allowed him to come into her shop and talk when she had removed her veil to do some of her work. She admitted that sewing was impossible to do with heavy gauze blocking the view. Even taking measurements and writing were probably a challenge. Several times, he'd seen her copying scriptures on a paper, and she never wore her veil for that, either.

The firm click of shoes on the hard floor alerted him to her approach. Quinn turned as Kathleen walked into the room. Disappointment flashed through him. Heavy green netting covered her face and part of her slender neck. An urge to rip the fragile material away made him clench his fists, lest he follow through with the desire. The beauty of her green dress stole his breath. The finely ruffled blouse over a straight skirt with ruffles at the hem and an overskirt of intricate ruffles and bows displayed her feminine charms. He could only imagine how the green of her dress would bring out the color in her eyes. What he wouldn't give to see them.

Kathleen paused. "Is there something wrong, Deputy?"

Quinn realized he still had a frown on his face from seeing her with her veil in place. He relaxed and smiled. "I had hoped you would accompany me without the veil. I can't imagine how hard it must be to have everything around you muted by the covering over your face. Can I convince you to leave it behind tonight?"

She stiffened. "I can see just fine. If my veil embarrasses you, we can cancel our plans for the evening."

"Oh, I'm not embarrassed. In fact, I was just considering my advantage over the other men in town."

"Your advantage?"

He reached to pluck his hat from the hat rack. His grin widened. "Of course. I'm the only single man in town who knows just how beautiful you are. The others don't have any idea how lucky I am."

"And just why are you so lucky, Deputy Kirby?" Her frosty tone almost made him glance up to see if snow was in the air.

"Why, because I'll be the gentleman at the fandango with the most beautiful woman on my arm. I know we got off to a rough start, but I think you have to admit to enjoying my visits."

Her slender hands clamped onto green-clad hips with

enough force to make Quinn wince. Pulling herself up to her full height, which meant the top of her head might reach his chest, Kathleen looked like she was prepared to wage a war.

"Oh, good. You two are ready to go." Glorianna swept into the room, a well-bundled baby in her arms. Conlon strode in behind her with the other twin snuggled on his shoulder.

"Good evening, Quinn." Glory stretched up and kissed his cheek. "Whoever would think I'd be so excited about a silly dance?" She sighed. "I've been cooped up here for weeks; and before that, I couldn't dance because I was so big, my husband couldn't get his arms around me."

"I believe you must be talking about someone else, my dear." Conlon gazed fondly at his wife. "I seem to remember my arms being around you a number of times."

Glorianna blushed. "If you two will help us with our cloaks, we'll be ready."

Quinn accepted the dark gray cloak Glorianna handed him and stepped toward Kathleen. She had relaxed her stance somewhat but still acted a bit miffed. He couldn't resist letting his hands linger a minute on her shoulders as he settled the cloak there. Giving her a little squeeze, he released Kathleen and stepped to her side.

"Shall we go?" Quinn offered his arm. Her head inclined to the right, and he thought he could see the faint shadow of a smile through the veil. Her slender fingers rested on his sleeve, their slight pressure making him long to see her expression clearly.

"Would you like me to carry that for you?" Quinn gestured at the satchel containing the babies' belongings. Conlon still hadn't figured out how to carry a baby, a satchel, and offer his arm to his wife. Quinn wondered how he would manage if he were in his friend's shoes. Before meeting Kathleen, he would have scoffed at taking the thought seriously. Now, the idea didn't scare him. Maybe being a husband and father could be right for him.

Although the fandango wasn't far, Conlon had arranged for a buggy to transport them. He told Quinn he wasn't sure Glorianna was up to walking so much yet. Besides, he wanted to have plenty of dances with his wife without her being worn out.

Strains of guitar and violin music drifted to them on the evening breeze long before they arrived. Cowhands and cavalrymen milled around the door, laughing and sharing stories as they watched the pretty girls inside. The men would be picking the one they wanted to dance with, then building courage before entering the hall.

Reaching up, Quinn put his hands on Kathleen's waist to swing her down. She must be made of air, because she sure didn't weigh anything. Once again, he chafed at the veil keeping him from seeing her expression. He thought maybe she enjoyed his company and his touch and longed to see for himself what her eyes would tell.

Kathleen hesitated as they faced the crowd of men around the door. She seemed to draw nearer to him. Quinn tightened his arm, pulling her close, wanting to comfort her.

"These men are noisy and a little rough sometimes, but they're harmless." Quinn leaned close, his cheek brushing her veil. He thought he could feel a slight tremor pass through her. "Shall we go on in?"

Conlon and Glorianna were disappearing through the group. Many of the cavalrymen called greetings to them. Kathleen stiffened her shoulders and nodded. Quinn led her in, not wanting to give her time to be afraid. She'd admitted to him a few days ago that being in public had been a rare occurrence in her life. He wondered if she was afraid of saying or doing something wrong. Perhaps she feared the careless remarks said by people who didn't stop to think before they spoke.

"Evenin', Deputy."

Quinn nodded at several of the young men crowding the door and returned a few greetings. Curiosity filled more than one gaze as the men parted to let them pass. Stifling a grin, Quinn again thought how lucky he was to have Kathleen at his side. He could feel the shaking of her hand on his arm and knew she would stick close simply because he was someone she knew and felt partially comfortable with.

Chattering women and uncomfortable-looking men crowded the inside of the hall. Most husbands would rather stay at home, relaxing for the evening. The women seemed to blossom in the charged social atmosphere.

At one end of the hall, several musicians seated on a raised platform tried out their various instruments. Even though they hadn't begun a formal song, the partial tunes they played made the people tap their toes, anxious for the dancing to begin.

A tug on his arm reminded Quinn that Kathleen stood beside him. He glanced down to find her gazing across the large room at a group of young women. Harriet and Maria, the new schoolteachers, stood with several other girls. Pulling his arm, Kathleen began to work her way through the crowd to reach her friends from the boardinghouse. Quinn hoped she didn't intend to stay with them all night.

By the time they reached the girls, the first strains of the opening song called the dancers to gather on the floor. Kathleen plucked the forgotten satchel with the babies' things from Quinn. Taking her hand from his arm, Kathleen pulled Maria forward.

"Maria, Quinn is dying to get started dancing. Would you mind joining him while I deliver these things to Glorianna?" With that she swept off, leaving a stunned deputy in her wake. Maria gave a shy smile, her brown eyes not meeting his as she stretched out her hand. As if in a dream, Quinn led her to the dance floor, his heart following the veiled beauty as she left him behind.

nine

"Here's the bag with the babies' necessities, Glory." Kathleen stepped into a small anteroom. Chairs were grouped in a corner, and several baby beds stood to one side of the floor. A few older ladies bent over some of the beds. Others sat with infants on their laps. At Kathleen's entrance, they looked up and seemed to realize for the first time that Glory and her twins were there. They rushed in an excited ensemble to surround the new mother and her sleeping newborns.

Glorianna handed Angelina to a stout, black-clad woman, then retrieved Andrew from Conlon, who made a hasty retreat. Handing Andrew, then the bag Kathleen carried, to the women, Glorianna drew her cousin to a corner of the room.

"What are you doing in here?" Glorianna looked suspicious. "Why aren't you with Quinn?"

"I had to bring you the babies' things." Kathleen breathed a quiet sigh of relief that Glory couldn't see her face. Even without the visual, Glory would probably know she was omitting something. Kathleen knew she couldn't hide what she'd done forever.

"Conlon is waiting for you out there. You'd better get a start on the dancing." Kathleen pushed Glory toward the door. Conlon turned, peering into the room. He pulled his wife onto the dance floor, where they began a lively step Kathleen had never seen.

After Glorianna disappeared from sight, Kathleen slipped into the nursery. She would do her best to hide here. Holding babies was much more to her liking than attempting to dance when she had no idea how to do such a thing. Her mother

71

...er to attend a function like this. There was ...ch chance that her mark would be seen and ...ily. Kathleen still felt uncomfortable appearing in p... ...n with her face covered.

Growing up, she met a few friends at church. Those friends kept her up on the latest happenings and romances in the community. They described picnics at the park, box socials, and dances in great detail, but Kathleen never experienced them in person. As a teenager she'd longed for a normal life, but now she was comfortable with the way things turned out. She didn't need love and marriage and family. She could be content with where God had her. Maybe the mark on her face was special to God.

"Look at this, Kathleen." Mrs. Monroy settled onto a chair beside her. Her plump cheeks creased as she smiled at Andrew nestled in her arms. "Have you ever seen such a sweet thing?"

"Not since looking at his sister." Kathleen grinned at the matron's startled expression.

Mrs. Monroy chuckled, her plump body shaking like jelly. "I reckon that's true. This has to be the prettiest pair of babies I've seen in years. Of course, with the parents they have, how could they be anything but beautiful? Glorianna and Conlon make a fine-looking couple."

Andrew scrunched his face in a scowl. Mrs. Monroy patted him until he burped and settled quietly to sleep. She snuggled the baby close and glanced over at Kathleen. "Of course, I'm wondering if there isn't another couple who look pretty good together."

"Is it someone I know?" Kathleen shot a glance at the door leading to the dance floor. Laughter and music drifted in, and she tamped down the longing to see the festivities.

"You're half of the couple, so I guess you know them." Mrs. Monroy smirked. Kathleen tried to keep her surprise from showing. "The other half is that handsome deputy sheriff who keeps showing up at my house. Funny thing is, I don't ever remember Quinn Kirby dropping by my place until you moved in. Now he's there every day."

A plump hand patted Kathleen's knee. "I don't know why you always wear that veil, Kathleen, but there are other ways of being beautiful than through one's looks. You have a caring, godly demeanor. Once these ladies get to know you, they can see for themselves what a beauty you are."

Once again someone was after her to rid herself of the veil. She knew Mrs. Monroy wasn't being bossy or nosy, she only intended to encourage and help. Kathleen wondered at the number of times she'd recently been asked to remove her veil. Always before, she spent most of her time around her family. She hadn't been alone with anyone long enough for them to care to look at her.

"I can't possibly take off my veil. People would stare and talk." Kathleen blurted out the truth before she could stop herself.

Mrs. Monroy's eyebrows shot skyward. "Take a look around you, Honey." She gestured to the women on the far side of the room. As soon as Kathleen looked their way, they acted as if they weren't watching her.

"You see, these women aren't used to seeing someone covered by a veil. They're all wondering what you have to hide. Believe me, the things they're imagining are probably much worse than the reality."

Kathleen's eyes burned. What were these people thinking of her? She hoped coming out West would be a new start for her, away from the gossip and memories of childhood. Maybe she couldn't escape the horror after all. Perhaps she should just return home and spend the rest of her life secreted in her mother's house. The thought of that miserable existence terrified her.

Mrs. Monroy eased up from the chair and stepped toward

the baby beds with the sleeping Andrew, then returned. "Whatever you're hiding, I know there will be some who might make crude remarks. You can't ever escape that, Honey, but the ones who count will accept you just the way the good Lord made you." Her hand cupped Kathleen's chin through the veil. "Give them a chance."

Watching Mrs. Monroy cross the room and join the other women seated in a group, Kathleen felt so alone. Her foot tapped out the beat of the music being played in the other room. Everyone but her seemed to have a place. All her life, she'd been an embarrassment to her family. Now she had no idea how to fit in with others. Glorianna interacted with the townspeople so naturally. Kathleen didn't think she could ever do that. She would always be aware of the mark on her cheek that set her apart from others. She would never be one with these people. Even now, she could still see the women casting glances in her direction and imagined the questions they were asking Mrs. Monroy.

"There you are, Kathleen. Why are you still in here?" Glorianna sank onto a chair beside her and wiped the perspiration from her brow. "Whew, the music is so fast here. I feel like I've run a few miles, and we've only done a few dances. I don't know how I'll make it through the evening." She grinned. "Of course, I'll figure out some way."

Reaching over, Glory grabbed Kathleen's hand and tugged. "Come on. I saw Quinn with one of the new schoolteachers, looking as uncomfortable as a man can. You have to come out there and rescue him."

"He's still with her?" Kathleen sat forward. A stab of jealousy cut through her. This was ridiculous. Her plan was working, and she didn't want it to. She forced her feelings to recede and tried to look on the positive side. "I think I'll stay here a little longer. I'm sure Quinn won't mind."

"Wait a minute. What's going on here?"

"Nothing. I was in here, talking to Mrs. Monroy." Attempting to look nonchalant, Kathleen relaxed in the chair. "Besides, next to you, I'm the woman who knows the twins best. My being in here assures you a much-needed evening with your husband. Now get out there before he comes looking for you."

Before Kathleen could react, Glorianna lifted the veil, pushing it up over her hat. "You are up to something, Kathleen, and I intend to find out what. You're not going to hide from me." Glory's eyes flashed as she stared into Kathleen's eyes. "Now you tell me why Quinn would bring you to this fandango, then spend the night dancing with other women."

Glancing across the room, Kathleen could see the ladies staring in their direction. She turned her head so they wouldn't be able to see her cheek and reached to lower the veil. Glory caught her hand.

"I told you, I can't allow Quinn to be interested in me. He's not a Christian. Letting him court me is just too dangerous." Kathleen twisted her skirt in her hand. "I decided to get him interested in some of the other available young women. Then he won't want to see me."

"Kathleen, Conlon and Quinn have done quite a bit of talking lately. Did you know Quinn was raised by Christian parents? The more I hear his story, the more I believe he's a lot like me. As a child, he thought he would get to heaven because of his family connections. Then, when things got tough, he didn't have the faith he needed to stand, so he turned away from God. I agree that you can't marry a nonbeliever, but I also believe God is working in Quinn's life."

"Don't you see? I can't take the chance of being around him." Kathleen choked and couldn't continue.

Tears glistened in Glory's eyes. "Because you already care too much for him. Am I right?"

She couldn't deny the truth any longer. Kathleen nodded. "You see, even if I were free to wed, I couldn't marry someone like him, an unbeliever."

Glorianna pulled her close and gave her a hug. "I understand. Conlon and I are praying for his salvation. God can do mighty works when you trust in Him. Look what He did for me."

❧

The line of dancers stretched before Quinn. They seemed to go on forever. Maria clung to his arm once again, smiling up at him whenever he looked her way. She was pretty, with dark hair piled high on her head and eyes that sparkled with merriment. He had seen the way some of the fellows from town watched her. Ed Fish, who rarely attended a social event, was here tonight. He hadn't taken his eyes off the schoolteacher but appeared too bashful to ask her to dance. Quinn groaned. Except for one time with Harriet, to the obvious jealousy of John Wasson, he'd spent the whole evening with Maria. He hadn't even had a glimpse of Kathleen since they'd arrived and she disappeared in the vicinity of the nursery.

He couldn't understand why Kathleen had paired him off with Maria. Although she was nice, he couldn't get her to say two words. She had to be intelligent, or she wouldn't be qualified to teach school, but so far he hadn't even learned where she hailed from. Dancing together, smiling at one another, and blushing occasionally weren't his ideas of an entertaining evening.

The music ended. In the moment of quiet he heard a soft voice. "I believe I'd like a cup of punch."

Quinn stared at the woman standing next to him. She'd spoken a whole sentence. He smiled. "Why don't you wait with your friends, and I'll see that you get some."

He escorted her across the floor to the gaggle of giggling young ladies, then departed. Working his way through the crowd, Quinn craned his neck, looking for the person he sought. Ed stood against the wall with John, talking and watching the proceedings. Weaving around some couples, Quinn approached them.

"Ed, I need a favor." The thin man didn't look happy to see him. He must think Quinn was trying to steal the girl he liked. "I need to find Kathleen. Would you take a cup of punch to Miss Wakefield and keep her company for awhile?"

Ed pushed off from the wall, his gaze straying to the group of girls across the room. "I reckon I can do that."

Quinn turned to leave, then halted. "John, I would imagine Miss Bolton might enjoy some, also. She seems to be a little tired."

The two friends strode off in the direction of the refreshment table. Quinn grimaced. Now he had to find the girl he came with and discover why she'd disappeared. Throughout the dancing he hadn't seen her in the hall one time. She must still be in the nursery with the babies. Usually only the older women stayed there. Why would Kathleen hide there this long? Was she that uncomfortable with people?

As he moved around the edge of the floor to avoid the dancers, Quinn returned greetings from many of the townspeople. Pondering the question of Kathleen's reason for hiding from him, he stopped at the door of the nursery room. Several women gathered across the room, their heads close together as they visited and laughed. He could hear someone speaking behind the open door and started to enter until he heard his name. Glorianna and Kathleen were talking about him. He recognized their voices. Quinn stilled, unsure whether he should leave or step into the room. He knew better than to eavesdrop, especially when he was the topic of conversation.

Before he could make a decision, he heard Kathleen's reason she was avoiding him. His lack of Christianity stood between them. Teeth clenched, he listened a moment longer. Quinn stalked to a side door and stepped outside. What difference did his beliefs make? He wouldn't keep Kathleen from believing the way she wanted. This was what he hated about Christians. If you weren't one of them, you weren't good enough. Well, he'd done just fine taking care of himself. Other than a few rough times, life treated him fine. Everyone had a few difficulties. It was to be expected.

When he realized he was pacing, Quinn forced himself to stop. The Christians he knew would use any form of trickery to get someone to accept their religion. Well, two could play at that game. What if he convinced Kathleen he believed the same as she did? He would have to be careful, but he could do it. Having been raised in a Christian household, he knew all of the lingo. He could pray with the best of them, spouting meaningless words that sounded spiritual.

Quinn moved into the open and stared up at the sky. He didn't know about God being real. God was for those who were weak and needed a crutch. He didn't need that, but he would convince Kathleen that he did. Turning to go into the hall, he ignored the prick of his conscience reminding him that men like Conlon weren't weak. Conlon recently told him he believed in Jesus because of the sin he committed—not because of a weakness. Sin could be a weakness of character, he argued silently. He didn't have that fault.

In a matter of minutes, Quinn stood in front of Kathleen. "I believe we have a dance to share." He held out his hand. She looked nervous, but accepted. To do otherwise would be rude. Leading her to the dance floor, he squeezed her hand. "I promise I'll go slow and teach you the steps. You'll be fine."

The music began, a slow melody designed to give the perspiring dancers a rest. Quinn drew her into his arms. "I know you miss having a church to attend." He ignored her start of surprise. "I heard from the wires today that a traveling evangelist is going to be here for a few weeks. I thought you'd like to go to the meetings with me."

Her sharp gasp and speechless silence were all the answer he needed. His plan was going to work.

ten

The feel of Quinn's hand on her back did disturbing things to Kathleen's equilibrium. She'd never been this close to a man other than the members of her family. The scent of soap and leather mingled together. A powerful longing to rest her head on his shoulder and surrender to the unnamed feelings sprang up inside her.

When he'd invited her to attend the evangelist meetings with him, she hadn't known what to say. Had she heard right? This independent, self-reliant man wanted to hear the Word of God? He would willingly accompany her? Somehow, his invitation didn't ring true; but she would go with him, if only to get him there. Glorianna mentioned she and Conlon had been praying for Quinn. That meant at least three people consistently prayed for his salvation. Maybe the preacher could bring the message that would touch Quinn's heart. The thought thrilled her.

"Are you always this quiet when you go out?" Quinn's low drawl close to her ear sent a shiver down her spine.

"I don't go out."

He drew away, staring at her veil as if he could see her face through the gauzy material. "What do you mean, you don't go out? Don't tell me you've never gone to a dance or at least a social of some sort."

She shook her head. "I didn't go many places when I lived at home. I went to church on Sunday morning and that was about all."

His eyes widened in amazement. "Why?"

Turning her head, Kathleen tried to think of a way to hide

79

the truth but couldn't. Quinn had seen what she looked like. Surely he would understand her mother's position and reasoning. "You should be able to guess, Deputy. I didn't want to disgrace my family."

His mouth dropped open, and he gaped for a few minutes before he spoke. "First off, I wish you would stop calling me Deputy. My name is Quinn, and you're welcome to use it."

His eyes snapped with anger. "Second, why would you disgrace your family? You're a kind, God-fearing person. The only thing you do that's shameful is wearing this veil to cover one of the prettiest faces I've ever seen."

This time her mouth fell open. "How can you say that? You've seen my face."

"If I remember right, there's nothing wrong with how you look. Your eyes could make a man lose his sense of direction." His face reddened and he grinned. "You've managed to make me lose my savvy. I don't know when I've paid a woman a compliment like this."

"Mr. Kirby." Kathleen paused when she saw the anger darken his eyes again. "Quinn. My parents had good standing in our community. Having a daughter with a mark on her face could have hurt their reputation. People are often unkind in what they say. My mother taught me early to cover my deformity so the family wouldn't be ostracized."

Quinn's arms tightened around her. She hadn't noticed how he was moving closer to the outer door each time they came around the floor until he swept her outside. As the last notes of the song faded, he released his tight hold but kept a firm grip on her hand.

"Let's walk for a minute. We need to talk." He growled out the words, a scowl wrinkling his forehead.

The cool night air felt good after the warmth inside. With all the dancers and crowds of people, the building had become stuffy. Kathleen took a deep breath of fresh air, trying to calm her jangling nerves. How could she explain her mother's actions to Quinn? Even Glorianna didn't understand.

"Are you telling me you've never attended a church social or been courted by a young man because your family might be embarrassed?" The muscles of Quinn's jaw clenched and loosened as he talked.

"Mr. K—Quinn, you mustn't think this was a terrible hardship. I'm glad to sacrifice for my family. I remember quite clearly the early years before Mother had the idea for me to be veiled. The children were horrible with their taunts. Sometimes they even resorted to violence against me."

The quiet stretched between them. Her fingers were becoming numb from Quinn's grip. She wasn't sure he even realized he held her hand.

"Didn't your father talk to the parents of the children who did this?"

Kathleen sighed. "That wouldn't have helped. You have to understand that the community we lived in was superstitious. Many times, people of all ages would cross to the other side of the street when they saw me coming. They kept their distance, as if the mark on me would rub off on them." She tried to keep the bitterness out of her voice.

"But the people of your church should have treated you right."

"Religious people tend to be easily swayed. They can be so eager to watch for Satan's traps that they see him everywhere rather than looking for God." Quinn nodded and she continued. "Many of the taunts and remarks made about me originated from the people in our church. Some of them believed I was marked by the devil. 'Satan's spawn' was a common jeer the boys yelled at me."

Quinn halted and pulled her around to face him. His eyes narrowed as he studied her. "I'd like to say I'm angry with your parents for not standing up for you, but I've experienced something similar. My sister too was the brunt of jokes and pranks. My father refused to do more than pray with her and teach her Scripture that said God loved her no matter what." He looked off down the street, his thoughts seeming to be far away. "I could never understand why God would allow someone like my sister to suffer so much."

Shaking his head, Quinn said, "I believe it's high time you experienced some of the things you missed as a girl. Tomorrow I'll come by for you. I want you to be dressed for a picnic. I know a beautiful spot down near the Santa Cruz River."

Kathleen couldn't think of an argument. A picnic. She'd always wanted to go on one. Excitement made her tremble. Maybe just this once she could agree to go with Quinn and fulfill her longtime dream. As a young girl, she used to picture going on an outing with a handsome man who made her laugh and feel beautiful.

The dance was winding down. People gathered their things, preparing to go home. Kathleen hurried inside to help Glorianna with the babies. She did her best to ignore the townspeople who stared at her as she worked her way through the crowd. No matter how many years she lived, she would never get used to everyone gawking as she passed by. If she removed her veil, would they stop ogling her as Mrs. Monroy suggested, or would they then begin to sling ugly comments along with the stares?

❧

"Ouch!" Kathleen pricked herself for the tenth time this morning. Picking up a rag, she quickly dabbed at the drop of blood. The tip of her finger had never been so sore. At this rate, she wouldn't have Mrs. Monroy's new dress done for another week.

What had possessed her last night to agree to go with Quinn? The romantic evening, dancing in his arms, and his sweet compliments all caused her to lose her common sense and agree to something dangerous. Even if Quinn were to become a solid Christian sharing a like faith with her, she couldn't marry him. She could never allow that. She shuddered to think of bringing a child into the world to suffer as much as she had.

All morning she'd prayed and tried to think of a way to get excused from this afternoon's outing. Yes, she would enjoy the picnic and seeing the river, but not with someone as attractive as Quinn. He made her lose her common sense. A sudden idea made her sit up straight in the chair. She folded the unfinished dress and placed it on the table beside her. This plan just might work.

&

Quinn stretched the wanted poster out and tacked it to the wall behind his desk. The bounty on the Veiled Widow just went up. She'd made her way to California, leaving two men dead and several more a lot poorer. The woman had to be stopped. What was the matter with the lawmen in the cities where she struck? Weren't they watching for her? Did she come to town without her disguise? If so, why couldn't anybody identify her? The only picture on the poster was that of a slender woman dressed in black, her face covered by a veil like the ones Kathleen often wore. This could be any woman.

He retrieved his hat from the rack and stepped outside. Señora Arvizu had prepared a basket lunch for him, and he'd made arrangements to rent a buggy from the stables. Whistling, he left to gather what he needed. He and Kathleen could have a picnic, and he would still be back in time to meet the evening stage. No one in Tucson could say Quinn Kirby wasn't doing his job. Protecting the citizens of this town was his first priority. A grin stretched across his face. Courting a certain hazel-eyed beauty was his second priority. He chuckled. Maybe even his third, fourth, and fifth priorities.

The smell of fried chicken wafted out of the basket next to

Quinn's feet as he drove the buggy to Mrs. Monroy's boarding-house and pulled to a stop. He jumped over the side, tied the horse, and strode up the sidewalk. He rapped on the front door, then fiddled with his hat as he waited for someone to answer. By the third knock, he realized no one was home or they were in a part of the house where they couldn't hear. Where was Kathleen? She'd said she would go with him. She'd even acted excited about the idea.

Quinn strode around the side of the house to Kathleen's shop. A bell trilled as he pushed the door open.

"I'll be with you in a minute." Kathleen's voice came from the adjoining room. She sounded a little winded. Quinn smiled. She was probably excited about the outing.

A few minutes passed before Kathleen entered the room accompanied by another younger woman, Luisa Espinosa. Quinn had seen her around town and knew her father but had never met Luisa. She appeared nervous, her hands fiddling with her skirt. Her long, dark hair was smoothed back and fastened with a bow. Long ringlets draped over her shoulders. Dark eyes peered from beneath long lashes, sought his, then glanced away. A deep gray dress hugged her slender figure, making him wonder about her age. She looked to be still in school, yet she seemed ready for a gentleman caller, so perfect were her dress and demeanor.

Kathleen, on the other hand, looked like she'd run out to the new fort and then home. Her hair straggled down in strands from the hat perched at an unnatural angle on her head. Wrinkles and a few stains marked her dress.

"Quinn, have you met Luisa?" Kathleen tried to straighten her hat and sweep up the falling tendrils of hair as she spoke. Her ministrations didn't meet with success. The instant she released her hold on the hat, it tilted sideways once more. Quinn longed to rip it off so he could see her with the shining locks falling around her face. He could imagine how charming she would look. For a moment his fingers ached to reach up and tug her hair free, allowing the heavy dark mass to float down around her shoulders. Would it fall to her waist?

"Quinn?"

He jumped. His face flamed. He'd forgotten her question.

"Quinn, are you all right?" At his nod, she asked again, "Have you met Luisa Espinosa?"

"I know her father. I've seen Luisa around town, but I don't believe we've been introduced before." He nodded at the young girl. "Pleased to meet you, Miss Espinosa."

"Luisa is here for a fitting. I'm making a dress for her and one for her mother. They want them done by next week. I also have to finish Mrs. Monroy's dress. She's talking about ordering another."

"Sounds like you're getting busy."

Kathleen's sewing business was taking off. He knew she would feel better about herself if she were able to make her own way in the world.

"The ladies here are very excited about getting the newest styles. Mrs. Monroy says they sometimes don't see the catalogs for two years after they've come out. I brought some with me, so several of the women in town have taken to dropping by and looking at the patterns."

Quinn mumbled something he hoped was appropriate. He couldn't understand women's fascination with fashion. Who cared whether you had the latest design or not? As long as the clothes fit and wore for a good length of time, what more did a person need?

"I'm told there are a couple of freighters in town who might be able to get me materials if I order by the bolt. Do you know them?"

"Of course." Quinn frowned, trying to decide who would be more likely to fill Kathleen's order. "Pinkney Tully and Estevan Ochoa would be the ones to talk to. Charles Lord and

Wheeler Williams do freighting, but theirs is mostly government contracts. They haul in a lot of the lumber and outfitting for the new fort."

"Then I'll seek out Mr. Tully and Mr. Ochoa tomorrow morning." Kathleen folded her hands in front of her.

"Are you ready for our outing?" Quinn didn't want to be rude, but he could picture some dog wandering down the street and smelling that basket full of chicken. There would go the lunch his stomach was calling for.

"Oh, the picnic." Kathleen's hands crossed over her breast. "I'm not at all ready to go. In fact, with all the work I've just been given, I don't know how I can get away right now." She pursed her lips as if she were thinking. Her hands clapped. "I know. You can take Luisa with you. That food shouldn't be wasted. Luisa, are you free to go?"

At the Mexican girl's bright smile and nod, Quinn knew he'd been set up again.

eleven

The last leg of chicken sat like a rock in the pit of Quinn's stomach. He glanced at the sweets Luisa popped into her mouth with great abandon and almost groaned. With maturity, Luisa would make some man a wonderful wife. Right now, she couldn't seem to think beyond the next meal to fix or the next dress to purchase.

"I just adore pink. Don't you, Deputy Kirby?" Luisa batted her impossible eyelashes and gave him a coquettish smile. "I believe I'll have Kathleen make me a gown of bright pink for next summer. With winter approaching, I prefer darker colors. Perhaps a red or even a burgundy. One with plenty of those fashionable satin ruffles. What do you think, Deputy?"

"I'm sure the young men will enjoy them. You'll be the belle at the next fandango for sure."

Luisa moved closer, careful not to leave the shade of the huge mesquite tree they rested under. "But what about you, Deputy? Will *you* enjoy seeing me in those dresses?"

Quinn tugged on the collar of his shirt. Glancing at the sun, he saw they hadn't been here nearly as long as it felt like. "I'm sure you'll be beautiful in any color, Miss Epinosa." He began to gather the food. "I hate to end the fun we're having, but I need to meet the evening stage."

Luisa laughed, a high-pitched giggle that grated like Patty McGregor's nails on the blackboard. "We have plenty of time, Quinn. You don't mind if I call you by your given name, do you?" He stared, speechless, and she continued. "The stage won't be in town for another two hours. That gives us the chance for a little stroll along the river." She simpered, "We have to do something after that delicious meal, don't we?"

Quinn rose and gave Luisa a helping hand up, trying to keep his disgust from showing. Kathleen would hear about this. He thought his plan to pretend to be a Christian was foolproof and she would fall for him in a minute. There must be some other obstacle to deal with before she would succumb. Gritting his teeth as Luisa sidled close and clung to his arm, he determined to discover the problem between him and Kathleen. He would let her know in no uncertain terms he wasn't looking for anyone else.

For another thirty minutes, he endured Luisa's chatter about clothing, styles, and colors. She talked about the fandango, how many boys she'd danced with, and how she would rather dance with him than any of them. Once she even knocked his hat into the river with her parasol. He had to clamber down the bank, soaking his best pair of boots in the process. All in all, his mood was foul and getting worse by the minute.

A steady drum of hoofbeats thundered on the road. Quinn peered toward town and saw a rider racing for them. Ed Fish pulled his big roan to a stop, scattering sand over Quinn's damp boots.

"Quinn, you got to hurry." The tall man was breathless with excitement.

Grabbing the reins of the prancing horse, dread raced through Quinn. He was Tucson's protector. What happened while he was out here wasting time?

"What is it, Ed?"

"One of Lord and Williams's wagons just pulled into town. They got attacked by Apaches and lost most of the men and all of the rigs but this one. Lord and Williams are in a bind. Those wagons carried all the supplies for the officers' housing in the new fort. The cavalry is being notified. They want to get a detachment ready to see what they can salvage."

Ed's horse pranced sideways, as if it sensed the excitement of the news. "The townspeople are riled up. They're talking about a posse. William Oury's trying to stir up trouble again."

"Ed, will you escort Miss Espinosa home for me? I'll take your horse." Quinn gestured downriver. "Our things and the buggy are in that stand of trees just down a ways. Luisa can show you."

Swinging down, Ed nodded to Luisa and offered her his arm. Quinn made his apologies and swung up onto the tall roan. As he raced away, guilt began to eat at him. He shouldn't feel so relieved when a tragedy was the reason he'd escaped such an uncomfortable situation. Never again would he escort Luisa Espinosa anywhere.

❧

A crowd of angry men surrounded the remaining Lord and Williams freight wagon as it stood in the street outside Doc Meyer's drugstore. The team of horses was being unhitched. Their heads hung low. Looking at them, Quinn wondered if they'd even make it to the livery where Lord and Williams kept their stock.

Without dismounting, Quinn faced the angry townsmen. "Boys, I want you to go home. I'll look into this matter, as will Lieutenant Sullivan from Fort Lowell. We'll get this resolved. If we need to deputize some of you to help out, we'll be letting you know."

"What about the woman?" one of the men shouted.

Quinn glanced around. "What woman?"

"The one who was injured." Manuel spoke up from the front of the crowd. "Doc Meyer has her inside, trying to fix her up."

"I didn't know a passenger was with the freight wagons." Quinn was puzzled. How had a lady come to be with the Lord and Williams party? "I still want you gentlemen to return to your work or homes. I'll check in with Doc Meyer. We'll make an announcement about what happened as soon as we know. You might watch for the article in the *Citizen*. I'm sure John will be reporting on this."

Grumbling and talking among themselves, the crowd broke into small groups and headed in different directions. A sigh of relief escaped Quinn. He could see William Oury glaring at him as the big man stalked off, surrounded by a few of his cronies. Quinn didn't want trouble. This would be a matter for the cavalry, and Conlon would be the one to get things going.

The door of the drugstore creaked as he stepped inside. He blinked, giving his eyes a moment to adjust to the dim interior before he moved toward the rooms where Doc Meyer saw patients. Usually, Charles Lord took care of the serious injuries, having been a physician in the Civil War, but he'd traveled east to make arrangements for more government contracts. When Dr. Lord wasn't in town, everyone's welfare fell to Charles Meyer.

Low voices spoke in hushed tones as Quinn entered the room. Conlon stood on one side of an examining table and Doc Meyer on the other side. A young woman lay between them, her face waxy, her appearance disheveled. She seemed to be unconscious. Blood soaked the right side of her dress from the shoulder to the waist. Doc Meyer was in the process of cutting away the sleeve and shoulder of her dress.

"Afternoon, Conlon, Doc. Who's this?"

Conlon's smile looked more like a grimace of pain as he glanced up at Quinn. Doc Meyer kept working.

"We're not sure who she is." Conlon's words were so soft, Quinn had to step closer to hear. "The driver said she talked to the head man about riding along with the train for safety purposes. He said she kept to herself and he hadn't even heard where she was headed for sure. She had a traveling companion—a younger woman who appeared to be a servant. The servant died in the attack. The men working with the train were told to stay away from her and her companion."

The three men studied the silent form as Doc exposed the wounded shoulder. He eased her up, exposing the exit hole for the bullet. Doc grunted. "At least I don't have to dig out a bullet. I'll get the wound cleaned and dressed. She should be fine in a few days. She'll be a little sore."

The woman groaned as Doc eased her down on the table. Sweat beaded on her forehead, but she didn't open her eyes. Her lips moved, but even when he put his ear close, Quinn couldn't make out what she tried to say. He figured she wasn't really aware of what was happening, but she wasn't all the way under, either. When Doc started working, she would probably lose consciousness completely.

Light brown waves of hair had once been pulled into a bun. Sometime during the attack or the flight afterwards, her hair had come loose. It now flowed down off the table. Lines creased the corners of her eyes. An old, jagged scar streaked across her right cheek, adding a mystique to her beauty. Her maroon traveling dress was ruined even before Doc cut the shoulder away. A maroon hat with a veil lay on the floor beside her. He assumed it had fallen there. Who was she? Why had she been traveling with freighters in dangerous territory? Where had the Lord and Williams train encountered her? Questions raced through Quinn's head at a dizzying pace with no answers forthcoming. He would have to wait to ask her until at least tomorrow. He knew Conlon had some inquiries of his own. The cavalry would need to know where the attack occurred and as much information as this woman and the driver could provide. Then they would be looking for this renegade band of Apaches.

૨૦

Chewing didn't help. The bite in Kathleen's mouth refused to be swallowed. A lump in her throat blocked the way. She couldn't understand how Quinn and Conlon could eat so calmly, as if nothing unusual had happened. . .as if several men and at least one woman hadn't died a violent death out in the desert. Another woman lay in the last room at Mrs. Monroy's, severely injured. If infection set in, she could die too.

The bite seemed to grow larger. Kathleen thought she would be sick if she didn't get it out of her mouth soon. Glorianna sat across from her, pale and silent, stirring her food on her plate. She, too, had been affected by the sad story of the attack. At least the twins slept. Babies and men. Maybe the two had something in common—the ability to shrug off catastrophic events. Then again, perhaps Conlon and Quinn had had more time to adjust to the horror. She knew they felt badly for the woman who lay wounded and unconscious. Comparing them to infants who had no knowledge of right or wrong hadn't been fair.

With a force of will, Kathleen swallowed. She could feel the slow path the bite took down her throat. Closing her eyes, she hoped it wouldn't want to come right back up. Pushing away her plate of food, she took a small sip of water.

"Did the woman have any belongings with her?" Glorianna's soft question came at a lull in the men's conversation.

"The driver said they didn't have time to gather anything. He said he whipped the horses to leave, and the woman jumped to grab the wagon. She was almost up when the bullet hit her shoulder. If he hadn't grabbed and pulled her aboard, the Indians would have killed her too. I don't think she even has a valise of her personal things." Conlon frowned. "Maybe when the men and I ride out there in the morning, we can recover some of her belongings."

"It would be nice to have her regain consciousness so we can find out some more about her and her companion. I'm sure there will be others to notify. Do you think she could have been traveling here to meet someone she knew or some family?" Quinn asked.

Conlon shrugged. "Hard to say. I haven't heard anything, but then I don't have the contact with townspeople the way you do."

"Well, I don't remember anyone saying anything about expecting relatives or company." Quinn drained his coffee. "I'd better get on patrol. I want to keep an eye on some of the men. There are those who would stir up trouble just for the sake of hunting down Indians, whether they've done anything or not."

Quinn's blue-gray gaze caught Kathleen, sending a jolt of awareness through her. He studied her, then looked at Glorianna. "I apologize, Ladies." Conlon seemed to follow his lead in noticing Kathleen and her cousin. His forehead furrowed.

"We've been talking about matters that are upsetting to you without thinking." Conlon reached across the table and cupped Glorianna's pale cheek. "I should have known when you were so quiet." He smiled, trying to lighten the mood. "We should have saved this discussion for later, when Quinn and I could be alone. You all right?"

A strand of Glorianna's hair tumbled down as she nodded. "I wish we could do something. Do you think Kathleen and I should take turns sitting with the woman? I'm sure Mrs. Monroy can't be there all the time."

"That's a fine idea, Sweetheart, but I think you've got plenty of your own to do. Andrew and Angelina might have something to say about you running off and leaving them— no matter how good the cause is."

"Let me get these dishes done, then I'll go right over and offer to sit with her." Kathleen rose and began to gather the plates. She hadn't meant to stay for supper, but she'd been helping Glorianna when Quinn and Conlon showed up with the news. Somehow they all ended up sitting down together, although only the men ate.

"You'll do no such thing." A bit of the old fire tinged Glorianna's tone. "The least I can do is wash up a few dishes. You go right on over and see how that woman is doing. When she wakes up, she'll need someone to be there to care for her."

"I'll walk you home." Quinn stood and reached for his hat. "I'd like to see if she's regained consciousness. Maybe she'll feel like talking a bit."

"Quinn Kirby, don't you dare tire that woman. She's been through enough."

Eyes widened, Quinn gave Glorianna an innocent look. "If she's too tired, I promise to hold off asking questions until tomorrow." He plunked his hat on his head and held out his arm to Kathleen. "Besides, Kathleen will be right there, watching to see that I behave myself."

"That's right." Kathleen bent over and kissed Glory's cheek. "Don't you worry about her. Just pray." She reached for her hat and veil, which she hadn't been wearing during the meal—proof that she was beginning to feel very comfortable with Quinn and Conlon.

A cool evening breeze made Kathleen draw her shawl closer. She hadn't expected to be out this late.

Quinn held her hand on his arm and tugged her close. Lifting her veil, he smoothed the gauzy covering over her hat. He moved around until he was gazing into her eyes. "There isn't anyone around, and I want to see your face. I believe you and I have some talking to do. I don't appreciate you sending me off with other women. I want to spend time with you, and I think we need to clear this up."

Kathleen felt a chill race through her that had nothing to do with the weather.

twelve

Through the cool night air, Quinn could feel Kathleen's hesitance. He knew she didn't want to talk about her deception. She was putting up a barrier between them, and he intended to bring it down before the wall grew too high to breach. This woman was special. She cared so much for other people. He could picture her being the kind of daughter-in-law his mother would love. She had spunk, but she also had compassion and a strong faith. Even though he didn't need the faith she believed in, he had no reservations about her clinging to her beliefs.

Moonlight peeked through the trees, bathing the ground with a golden glow. The night brought quiet to this part of Tucson that was rarely disturbed. Most of the action was closer to the downtown area where the businesses were. Quinn knew he couldn't stay here long. He needed to check on the men and make sure they weren't getting stirred up unnecessarily. Walking slowly, he tried to sort his thoughts before he began.

He cleared his throat, the sound loud and coarse in the darkness. Kathleen started. He patted her hand. "I want to know why you agree to do something with me, then back out. At the fandango, you ran off and left me dancing with Maria. Today, you promised to attend a picnic with me, something you've never done with anyone before. When I came to pick you up, you had Luisa ready to go."

He could almost see Kathleen cringing at his words, but he refused to stop. "When I ask you to go somewhere with me, it's you I want to spend time with—not anyone else. I believe

95

you've enjoyed my company. Perhaps I'm wrong, though. Are you trying to say you don't have feelings for me?"

Her head bowed as if she were mulling over her answer. Silence stretched between them as they strolled closer to the boardinghouse.

"I do enjoy your company." Kathleen tugged on her hand, which he held fast. "No matter what I feel for you, this relationship can't go anywhere other than with us as friends." Quinn thought he caught a glimmer of tears in her eyes as she met his gaze for a moment.

"Why do you say that?"

"Because we have different convictions. I follow what the Bible teaches. God says I shouldn't be yoked with an unbeliever."

"So you're saying I'm an unbeliever and not worthy of you? Isn't that a harsh judgment on your part?"

Kathleen drew back as if she'd been struck. Her eyes widened. "I'm not the one passing judgment. I'm only repeating what you've said yourself."

Knowing he had to step carefully to convince Kathleen of his sincerity, Quinn thought a long moment before he spoke. "I was raised to go to church. I've read the Bible and know who God is and what He expects of His children. I do believe in God, but I also believe in the goodness of His creation, mankind. I believe God put us here on earth, and what we do with our lives is up to us. We can live right, which I think I'm doing a good job of; or we can live wrong, like a lot of folks do. I don't see that I'm any different from you."

He hadn't meant to talk so long. Convincing Kathleen they were compatible in religious matters might be more difficult than he expected, considering the hesitant look on her face. Going to hear the evangelist should show her he was right with God. After all, how did God have time or energy to direct the lives of everyone on earth? Did He really care enough to do that?

"There's another reason we can't be more than friends." Kathleen halted at the porch of Mrs. Monroy's house. She touched the mark on her cheek. "I can never marry and have children. Passing on something like this to a child would be cruel beyond measure. I can't do that."

Sadness made Quinn's heart break. "I have no idea who taught you such nonsense, Kathleen." His fingers skimmed across the chocolate mark on her cheek. "There is nothing wrong with you. Besides, there is no guarantee you would pass this on. Do either of your parents have one? Do any of your sisters or brothers?" She shook her head, her eyes lowered.

"I didn't think so. You may have a passel of children and not one of them would share that mark with you. Or, you may have one or more that do. It wouldn't matter to me. I would love them even more if they carried that part of you."

She stopped cold. "How can you say that? You have no idea what life is like when you're different. People are cruel, especially children. As long as I have a choice, I will never subject a child to the kind of life I've lived. Never."

Swiveling around, Kathleen jerked her hand from his arm. She pulled the veil over her face and ran to the door before he could stop her. Quinn didn't know whether to follow her or let her think for awhile and talk to her in the morning. A rapid succession of gunshots made the decision for him. Things were heating up downtown. He'd better make an appearance and try to cool some tempers before someone got hurt.

૨૦

The front door pressed against Kathleen's back as she waited to see what Quinn would do. An overpowering longing to have him come after her, declare he could make everything right, and tell her how much he loved her weakened her knees until she thought she might collapse. *Lord, why am I so attracted to this man? I tell him how I don't ever want*

children and why, but that's more to convince myself than
him. I do want children, Lord. I love to hold Andrew and
Angelina. You know how sometimes I pretend they're my
own. I'm so confused. I don't know what You want me to do.

Tears dripped onto her dress, leaving dark spots in the fabric. Exhaustion claimed her. Kathleen started to push away from the door when a volley of gunshots echoed from far away. Fear stilled her. Quinn. The commotion would draw him to his job. A sudden image of Quinn facing a mob of angry, armed men made her gasp. What if he were hurt? Or worse, what if he were killed?

Whirling around, she struggled to pull open the door. Her fingers, still wet from wiping away tears, slipped on the knob. With a cry of exasperation, Kathleen wrenched the door open. She rushed onto the porch, her eyes straining to adjust to the darkness. She could hear the pounding of footsteps moving fast, far down the street toward the center of town. She knew Quinn raced headlong into danger, heedless of what might happen. He believed keeping peace in this community to be his utmost responsibility, and nothing would keep him from his job. Wrapping her arms around her waist, she prayed for his safety, but mostly for his salvation. From their troubling discussion tonight, she knew he didn't fully comprehend God's plan of salvation. She hadn't felt the timing was right to share Bible teachings with him since he was so adamant about his beliefs. Now, she prayed for a softening of his heart so he would be willing to listen when God's Spirit spoke.

The night's soft breeze dried the wetness from her cheeks. She began to shiver and knew she needed to get out of the cool air. The low babble of voices in the parlor greeted her as she shut the door. Maria peered into the hall.

"There you are, Kathleen. We heard the door a few minutes ago and thought you were here, but you didn't come in.

Then we heard the latch click and were just wondering if there were haunts at work." Maria's smile warmed Kathleen.

"I did come in, but then I heard some gunshots and stepped outside to see if Quinn was still here." Kathleen tried to keep the shaking from her voice. "He'd already gone."

Harriet stepped up beside Maria. "I imagine he has to stop some revelry that's gotten out of hand." She shivered and crossed her arms over her bosom. "I'll pray the Lord keeps him safe."

"Thank you." Warmth surrounded Kathleen, making the chill of the day's events ease. "How is the woman Quinn and Conlon brought here? Has she regained consciousness?"

Sadness filled Maria's eyes. "She's still not awake. Mrs. Monroy has been sitting with her most of the evening. We were going over our lesson plans for tomorrow, then hoped to take a turn with her."

"Don't worry." Kathleen held up her hand, palm outward. "I can gather some of my sewing and do my work right in her room. You get your school lessons planned." She smiled. "Besides, you two need your rest. It's hard to imagine being in charge of all those children when you're refreshed, let alone when you're tired."

After she'd grabbed a basket from her sewing room, Kathleen filled it with the dress she was working on and all the thread and necessities. Much of the evening had passed, but she knew she couldn't sleep now anyway. After hearing of the day's events and thinking about the crisis Quinn faced, she might be awake for hours.

Mrs. Monroy sat in a rocking chair next to the bed, her knitting needles held motionless in her lap. Her ample chin tilted down. Soft snores vibrated in the air. The woman on the bed lay still and pale as death. Brown, wavy hair fanned out on the white pillow beneath her head. Kathleen stared for a long moment, frozen in the doorway, until she saw the slight movement of the sheet covering the woman's chest. She still lived.

Giving herself a mental shake, Kathleen moved into the room to waken Mrs. Monroy. Quinn had told her and Glorianna that Doc Meyer had confidence the woman would be fine, but a gunshot and bleeding could never be scoffed at. This woman hadn't received immediate attention because of the harrowing ride to town on the racing wagon. Even though the ride saved her life, the jolting must have cost blood she couldn't spare.

"Mrs. Monroy." Kathleen gave the woman's shoulder a gentle shake. "Mrs. Monroy."

The older woman snorted awake, her fingers taking up the knitting needles as if she'd never stopped working. Sleep-laden eyes gave Kathleen an uncomprehending look.

"Mrs. Monroy, I've come to sit for awhile. Why don't you go on to bed?" Kathleen lifted the basket. "I'm wide awake and have some sewing to work on."

Heaving up from the rocker, Mrs. Monroy groaned as her joints popped. "Thank you, Kathleen. I haven't heard a peep from the lady. She seems to be resting fine. I couldn't find any evidence of a fever." The older woman walked with mincing steps to the door, leaned against it, and looked back at Kathleen. "If she needs something, don't hesitate to wake me. I'll be right down the hall. I have some broth in the warmer of the stove if she needs something to eat. Doc says not to give her regular food right away."

"Don't you worry. We'll be fine." As Mrs. Monroy shut the door behind her, Kathleen set the basket of sewing beside the rocker and crossed to the bed. She gave the woman's forehead a light touch but found no fever. Her steady breathing sounded clear.

A jagged scar stood out in bright relief on her pale cheek. Kathleen touched the old wound with her fingertip. What had happened to make such a scar? Had she been young then or was this a more recent mishap? Her features were pretty, but Kathleen noticed the hat and veil on the dresser. Had she too hidden her shame behind a veil?

Kathleen settled into a rocker and pulled the dress onto her lap as she listened to the woman's soft, steady breathing. The lamp on the table next to the chair gave plenty of light to see for stitching seams. The finer work would have to wait until daylight. Time sped by as she went from thinking of her growing feelings for Quinn and the dangers involved with loving him to wondering how her family fared and if they missed her. She missed her younger siblings, but being out from under her mother's negative influence had only been a relief. Guilt consumed her when she acknowledged those feelings.

Silence settled over the house as Maria and Harriet checked on Kathleen, then headed off to bed. A brisk wind rattled the windowpanes on occasion. Kathleen found herself straining to hear more gunshots as her thoughts continually strayed to Quinn. Every unusual noise set her nerves on edge.

When she pricked her finger for the fourth time because she kept drifting to sleep, Kathleen folded the dress and placed it back in the basket. She glanced a final time at the still figure on the bed, lowered the lamp wick, and rested against the rocker. Her heavy eyelids refused to stay open any longer. Peace stole over her as she drifted off to sleep.

"Water."

The hoarse whisper startled Kathleen awake. She glanced around the darkened room, wondering where she was.

"Water." The woman on the bed stirred and moaned as if the movement caused her great pain.

Raising the wick on the lamp, Kathleen crossed to the bed. Mrs. Monroy had set a pitcher of water and a cup on a night table. Kathleen lifted the woman's head, helping her to get some of the precious liquid into her dry mouth. After a few sips, the woman nodded that she'd had enough. A sigh, probably of relief, escaped as Kathleen lowered her onto the bed.

"Thank you." She sounded stronger and gave a wan smile.

"I'm sorry if I hurt you." Kathleen straightened the covers. Taking a damp cloth, she wiped the woman's brow and checked her for fever even though her clear eyes denied any weakness.

"What happened?" The woman grimaced as she tried to move.

"Stay still." Kathleen rested her hand lightly on the woman's uninjured shoulder. "Your party was attacked by Indians. You were shot. The doctor already cleaned your wound and says you'll be as good as new in a few days. Do you remember any of what happened? Can you tell me your name?"

Pale blue eyes gazed at Kathleen. Panic made her eyes brighten. She started to rise up off the bed, and her face paled with the effort. She fell back with a moan. "Cassie. What happened to Cassie? Where is she?"

Sorrow closed Kathleen's throat, making speech difficult. She swallowed. "Is Cassie the girl traveling with you?" The woman nodded. Kathleen wished anyone else were here to relay the sad news. "The man who brought you in said the other woman died. You and the driver were the only ones who survived the attack."

"No." The cry echoed through the small room. Turning her head away, the woman wept. Silent tears streamed down her cheeks.

thirteen

A light knock preceded Quinn poking his head around the door of Kathleen's shop the next morning. Eyes gritty from lack of sleep, Kathleen gave him what she knew had to be a tired smile. She couldn't even muster up a giddy feeling of relief to see him alive after the uncertainty of last night. Before dawn this morning, the woman, who finally identified herself as Edith Barstow, had fallen into a fitful sleep. She'd insisted on Kathleen repeating everything she knew of the attack and of the cavalry's plans to recover the bodies and belongings this morning. After Edith had fallen asleep, Kathleen barely managed to drag herself to her own room. She'd dropped onto her bed fully clothed and fallen asleep before she could pull up the covers.

"Morning. You look a little tired."

"I've had nights with more sleep." Kathleen rotated her shoulders, trying to ease the stiffness. "In fact, most nights have included more rest." She gestured at a chair. "Come on in."

Settling into the chair beside hers, Quinn reached out and took her hand. "Thank you." His blue-gray gaze held hers.

"For what?" She couldn't imagine what she'd done that made him want to thank her.

"For this." He reached out and traced her bare cheek, sending a tingle through her.

"I. . .I guess I'm so tired, I forgot." Kathleen glanced at the veil on the table with her sewing.

"Maybe you're getting used to me and don't think you need to hide anymore." Quinn smiled. Kathleen couldn't breathe. She couldn't think of a reply. For a moment she couldn't even recall why she wore a veil.

Quinn blinked. The air seemed to lighten. Kathleen felt her face flush and wished she had her veil on to hide the redness. Did he know how much his presence affected her?

"I heard the gunshots last night." Kathleen picked up her sewing from her lap, concentrating on the stitches. "Is everyone all right?"

"There was a little trouble down at the saloon. Some of the boys got to arguing about who should do what to the renegades, and shots were exchanged. No one got hurt. I guess it was their way of letting off steam." He crossed his legs at the ankles. From the corner of her eye, Kathleen could see him watching her with a smug sort of smile on his face.

"Were you worried?"

She pricked her finger. Yanking the injured digit away from the needle, she stalled for time. "I thought maybe the men would try to take vengeance themselves. Remember, you once told me about the lynchings that happened a year ago or so? I didn't know how they would take to the news of what happened yesterday." She found herself reluctant to say anything about the actual attacks. The horror, relived with Edith last night, lay fresh on her mind.

"William Oury is the main one I'm worried about." Quinn's eyes turned hard. "That man is good at organizing and getting people to do what they wouldn't normally do."

"I don't believe I've met him."

"He was at the dance the other night." Quinn seemed almost angry at the thought. "He's a big man, with a long, dour face. William always looks like he's just sucked on an early lemon."

"I take it this William is not one of your favorite people."

Quinn sighed. "I know my parents used to preach forgive and forget, but sometimes the wrongs people do shouldn't be forgotten. If you forget the evil, then you may not be ready to stop them from doing the same again."

Surprise made Kathleen pause in her work. She'd never seen Quinn so angry. Although he still looked relaxed, he was actually as tense as a cat ready to pounce. What had Oury done to warrant this kind of dislike? She wasn't sure she wanted to know.

"Back in '70 and '71, the Apaches were causing a lot of trouble." Although Quinn spoke, his eyes had such a faraway look, Kathleen didn't think he was in the room with her. She stitched while he continued. "There were a lot of raids. Ranchers and farmers outside of Tucson were hit the hardest. The townsfolk didn't get attacked because of the number of people here.

"William Oury led a party to Florence to see General Stoneman about getting help. The general said there weren't enough people in the Santa Cruz valley to warrant a cavalry troop coming down here."

Kathleen gasped. "You mean he didn't even try to help out?"

"Nope." Quinn frowned. "The raids continued. People died. Oury and some of his friends were angry. I can't fault them for that." He stopped and met her eyes. "I don't agree that the Indians were right to do the raiding and killing, but what Oury did was worse than that."

"What could be worse than killing innocent people?"

"In the spring of '71, Oury led a party of men, mostly Papagos, up to Aravaipa Canyon near Camp Grant. A group of Apaches had come to the camp, seeking refuge. The camp commander vouched for them and said they weren't responsible for the trouble."

"Mr. Oury wouldn't believe the commander?"

"I don't know why, but he decided these were the Indians responsible for all the troubles of the people in this valley. He led almost one hundred and fifty men on a dawn raid of the village."

"Didn't the cavalry troops at Camp Grant try to stop them?"

Quinn shook his head. His eyes sparked with anger. "The Apaches set up camp several miles up the creek from Camp Grant. The commander had no idea of the raid until it was over." He rubbed his eyes. Kathleen clutched the material, her sewing all but forgotten.

"All the young men were gone on a hunting expedition. Oury and his men waged war on women, children, and a few old men."

"Surely they stopped when they realized the men they thought responsible weren't there." Ice raced up Kathleen's arms. She shivered and wished for something to take the chill away.

"I told you what they did was worse than anything the Indians did. Oury and his men killed and mutilated most of the tribe. What they did to the women isn't something I can tell." He stopped, a pained expression making him look sick. "The children who weren't killed were taken captive so the Papagos could sell them as slaves."

"No." Kathleen's hand flew to her throat. "We fought a war against slavery. How could that happen?"

"That war was in the States. Arizona is a territory, and slavery among captives has been a part of Indian life for generations. Before anyone knew what happened, those twenty-eight children were already sold and taken to other places."

"Were Mr. Oury and his men punished?"

Quinn gave a harsh laugh. "Oh, they went on trial all right. The raid happened in the spring of '71, and they went on trial in December. It took the jury a whole nineteen minutes to decide they were innocent of all charges. The whole trial was a travesty of justice."

Kathleen blinked. Her eyes burned as she thought of the horrible deaths suffered because of this man and his perverted sense of justice. Quinn's hand closed over hers. She hadn't even heard him move. He raised her hand to his lips and kissed her fingers.

"I'm sorry. I shouldn't have told you that story. After yesterday's attack, I worry about what Oury will do. Conlon believes the man will let the cavalry handle the matter. I hope he's right."

A shudder raced through Kathleen. Quinn tightened his grip, his thumb tracing a path across her knuckles. She fought to keep from leaning toward him. Never had she wanted to be held as much as she did now. The desire to feel Quinn's arms around her, comforting her, strengthening her, almost overwhelmed her good sense.

❧

Guilt filled Quinn. Why did he tell Kathleen that story? What was there about her that made him want to bare his soul? He knew the answer to that one. She not only listened; she cared. He couldn't remember meeting anyone except his mother who had such compassion. Kathleen saw what others needed or wanted, and she reached out to them. Even with a birthmark she considered a handicap, she still thought of everyone else before she thought of herself. His father had talked to him many times about that trait as being one Jesus demonstrated. Compassion for certain people came easily for Quinn. Men like Oury didn't deserve forgiveness or caring.

Kathleen's hands still trembled in his. They felt like ice, as if she were frozen from the inside out. He knew rubbing his thumbs over her knuckles wasn't enough to warm her. She needed a distraction.

"I almost forgot the main reason I came by this morning." He smiled, hoping to ease her discomfort.

"What's that?"

"I wanted to see if the woman we brought over yesterday had regained consciousness."

Nodding, Kathleen drew her hands from his. "She woke in

the middle of the night. Her name is Edith Barstow. She's very bewildered. I had to tell her what happened."

"She didn't remember the attack?"

"She remembered parts of it. Her shoulder was causing her so much pain. Doc Meyer had given her something that might have left her confused too. Anyway, after I mentioned the attack, she began asking for the girl traveling with her, Cassie."

"Cassie who?"

"She didn't give a last name. For hours she cried and moaned. I thought she might be getting a fever, but she didn't feel hot. Finally, just before dawn, she dropped off to sleep."

"I'll need to talk to her as soon as I can."

"Why don't you wait here. I'll see if she's awake." Kathleen put on her hat and adjusted her veil before slipping from the room. In a few minutes she returned and beckoned to Quinn. "Mrs. Monroy gave her permission for you to go to Edith's room although men are not usually allowed beyond the sitting room. This is a special circumstance since Edith is still too weak to get up."

The door to the woman's bedroom flew open as they approached. Mrs. Monroy came out, carrying a tray with dishes stacked on it. She leveled a stare at Quinn. "Deputy, Edith has been through a lot. I don't want you tiring her. Understand?"

Feeling like a schoolboy called up in front of the class, Quinn nodded. "I'll do my best, Mrs. Monroy. Kathleen will be there to make sure I don't ask too many questions."

Edith Barstow looked thinner than he remembered from yesterday. A strong breeze could blow her away. Although she had a trace of pink in her cheeks, her color almost matched that of the sheets. Her nightdress showed dark traces of bloodstains. The wound had bled through the bandage at some time during the night. The white line around her mouth told of her pain.

"Miss Barstow, this is Deputy Quinn Kirby. He'd like to

ask you a few questions." Kathleen smoothed the hair from Edith's brow. Edith's pale eyes turned to him.

"Good morning, Miss Barstow. I'm sorry to bother you, but I need to find out what happened as soon as possible. I'm working with the cavalry, and we'd like to catch the party responsible."

A tear traced a path down her pale cheek, following the jagged line of the scar. "You're too late, Deputy. Cassie's dead. There's nothing you can do to help that."

"Can you tell me who Cassie was?"

"She was my sister." Quinn bent down to hear the whispered reply. "We'd just gotten together and were traveling to Tucson to begin a new life. Now she's gone. I tried so hard." She choked and turned her head away. An involuntary cry of pain escaped as she moved the injured shoulder.

Kneeling by the bed, Kathleen clasped Edith's hand in hers. "Can you tell Deputy Kirby about the attack, Edith? Any details you can remember will help."

Edith's chest jerked as a sob wrenched from her. "I'll try. There were so many of them. They were everywhere at once. We had just finished taking a break so the horses could have some water and a rest. That was to be the final stop before we reached Tucson. We were so close." She covered her mouth with her hand, as if to hold back the horror.

"That's fine, Miss Barstow." Quinn squeezed the rim of his hat. "Why don't you relax, and I'll talk to you later. I'll be riding out to the site of the attack with Lieutenant Sullivan and a troop of cavalrymen."

She brought her head around to stare at him with tear-drenched eyes. "Cassie. . . Will you see to her? I can't bear the thought of her lying there like that." Another sob shook her, making her face lose the bit of color she had.

"We'll see that she gets a proper burial, Miss Barstow. Don't you worry about that." Quinn slipped his hat on and caught Kathleen's attention. He motioned toward the door and she nodded.

"I'll walk Deputy Kirby out, then come back to sit with you, Edith. Is there anything you need?" Edith shook her head, and Kathleen rose to precede Quinn from the room.

In her shop, Kathleen brushed the gauze from her face and began to gather some of her sewing together, placing what she needed in a basket. Quinn could see the dark circles of fatigue around her eyes.

"Don't you think you should get some sleep before you sit with her again? I'm sure Mrs. Monroy would be happy to do that while you nap."

Kathleen gave him a tired smile and shook her head. "After all that woman has been through, the least I can do is lose a little sleep." She paused, toying with a thimble. "I felt so badly for her last night. She kept repeating how she and Cassie had gotten together and were starting a new life. I didn't know they were sisters."

"I wonder what she meant by that?"

"I don't know. She just kept saying, 'I worked so hard to get her free, and now it was all for nothing.'" Kathleen looked at him, a frown wrinkling her forehead. "I kept wondering why Cassie wasn't free before."

Quinn shrugged and reached for the door. He had to leave before he couldn't resist the urge to pull Kathleen into his arms and try to erase the tired look from her eyes. "That sounds like quite a mystery." He gave her a saucy wink that he hoped set her heart pounding and stepped out into the sunshine.

fourteen

Quinn sat at his desk, his head resting in his hands, staring blankly at a wrinkled wanted poster. He'd failed. His job in this town was to protect the citizens. From the talk in town and the nervous way the townspeople acted, he knew they were all upset about the raid on the freight wagons. There hadn't been an Indian attack for over a year now, but this one shook everyone. Deep down, he knew preventing Indian uprisings wasn't his responsibility, but he still felt guilty.

This also shook the foundation of his beliefs. He'd already berated himself for holding the conviction that he could take care of most anything. Lately, he hadn't been able to prevent a lot from happening. As he thought about his trust in the goodness of mankind, now he wondered how he could have allowed such a delusion. The actions of men like William Oury, who butchered innocent people and justified—even bragged—about what they had done, shook his faith. Even the Indian attacks showed the worst in man, didn't they? After they'd lived peacefully for so long, why did the Indians take innocent lives? Where was the goodness in that?

Quinn scrubbed his hands over his face. Stubbornness rose up inside him. His beliefs were right. Time had proved that mankind was basically good. Look at Kathleen, Glorianna, and Mrs. Monroy. They were charitable people. What about Conlon? Quinn couldn't ask for a better friend. He pushed away from his desk and stood. Just because a few people had no redeeming qualities in them or had moments of weakness, didn't mean everyone was evil. He had to cling to that. After all, for the last eight years of his life, that idea had carried him through most anything. He refused to let himself be deluded .

He plucked the poster from his desk and turned to tack the picture next to the poster of the Veiled Widow on the wall. The woman seemed to stare out at him, the mocking smirk on her face hidden by the dark covering. Still, he knew the taunt was there. She thought no one would find her, but she was wrong. Someday she would make the mistake of coming to this town, and he would be waiting. He could feel her evil in his bones. She was close, and he had to be ready.

The door swept open. Early morning chill rushed in as Conlon stepped through. "The men are waiting for us. You about ready to go?" Conlon's serious expression told of the grimness of the expedition. They were riding out this morning to bury the bodies of those killed in the attack and recover any belongings they could.

Quinn couldn't help the heaviness weighing him down as he followed his friend out the door. Riding out of town, the cavalry troop stayed silent as if they were already displaying a respect for the dead. Even the clink of bridles and the creak of leather sounded loud in the early quiet. At the end of the column, a wagon loaded with shovels and picks lumbered after them.

Vultures wheeling in lazy circles marked the site of the attack. The men could see their destination long before the grisly scene came into view. Most of them covered their mouths and noses with their neck scarves. Despite the relatively weak winter sun, the smell wasn't pleasant.

Conlon split up the men, directing some to begin digging graves while others would help gather any salvageable belongings. They would trade off jobs to relieve those using shovels in the difficult desert soil.

Quinn followed Conlon past the bodies of teamsters, some with arrows still protruding from them, most dead from gunshot wounds. Quinn knew that, like him, Conlon searched for

Edith's sister. What if the woman hadn't been killed during the attack? What if the Indians had taken her captive? Would they be able to rescue her? A shiver ran down his spine as he recalled the stories of the Oatman family who was attacked by Mohave Indians in 1851. The two girls survived the attack and were taken captive. Years later, their brother rescued Olive from the Indians. Her sister died in captivity. Olive's beauty was ruined by the facial tatoos the Indians forced on her. He could only imagine the horror she had lived through. He didn't want Miss Barstow's sister to have to suffer in a similar way.

"Here, Quinn." Conlon stopped on the other side of a group of rocks. His face paled under his tan.

The sour taste of bile filled Quinn's mouth. He'd seen death plenty of times, but the young girl sprawled on the ground beside the rocks was the worst. She couldn't have been much older than his sister. Even in death, her face bore a look of innocence. The gunshot through her chest must have caused an instant death. Quinn breathed a sigh of thanks for that.

"Look at this." Conlon motioned to her arm and her neck where the dress had torn. Greenish-yellow bruises marred her skin. Conlon frowned. "Someone hasn't treated this girl right."

Quinn shuddered. "Who would do such a thing? She looks as if she's been choked and beaten sometime in the last few weeks." A shawl lay on the ground near the girl. Quinn picked it up and covered her exposed limbs the best he could.

"We'd best have some of the men move her down to the burial site. Then we can start looking for any belongings the Indians left behind. I'm hoping to find the bags these two women were carrying."

"I've thought of that too." Quinn nodded in agreement. "Miss Barstow will feel a little better if we can find something of her sister's for her to hang on to."

For the next hour, Quinn and Conlon searched through the goods strewn across the landscape. Most of the foodstuffs had disappeared, and the other things were badly damaged or destroyed. Some of the wagon pieces had been piled together and set afire. A pall of smoke still hung heavy in the air, making Quinn's throat ache long before they finished their search.

"Here, Sir." One of Conlon's men gestured from across the battle scene. They hurried over, slipping on the rocky ground.

"Would these be the ladies' bags, Sir?" The soldier gestured to two valises, their sides scraped and covered with dirt. "I found them under the pieces of this dresser. This must have fallen off a wagon and covered the bags. No one saw them."

Conlon knelt down and opened the closest satchel. A pile of feminine clothing, scented with a faint lavender, showed these indeed belonged to Miss Barstow or her sister. Conlon straightened.

"Thank you, Kent." He nodded to the young soldier. "Why don't you load these on the wagon, and we'll see that they get to Miss Barstow when we return to town."

Kent carried the two satchels down the hillside. Conlon and Quinn gazed at the wreckage around them. Many of the articles had been furniture items for the new fort. This would set them back as they waited for more to be shipped.

Conlon gathered what little sign of the Indians he could find. He and Quinn discovered where the raiding party had approached the unsuspecting wagon train and where they rode off after the raid, their horses heavier for all the extra food they carried. All the teams were missing too—probably taken by the Indians.

"Ready to go?" Conlon looked as gritty as Quinn felt. They watched the column of smoke from the burning goods ascend. "I could use a bath and some cool water." A sad smile creased Conlon's face. "I could also use some time with my family. Somehow, after seeing something so horrible, I always want to hold Glory and now the babies too." He acted embarrassed at having said something so personal. "I suppose that sounds funny to you."

"Not at all." Quinn swung up into the saddle. "The only thing that's kept me going this last hour is the thought that I'll get to see Kathleen this evening." He could feel his face flush and wondered at his temerity in letting Conlon know of his interest in Glorianna's cousin.

"You two getting pretty close?" Conlon signaled for the men to fall in behind them as they moved out into the road.

Heat ran down into Quinn's collar. "I just admire her spunk. She's been through a lot and is the most caring person I've ever met. In her shoes, I think I might have ended up bitter and angry at the world."

"That's true." Conlon frowned. "From what Glory's told me, Kathleen went through a lot with the people in their neighborhood, but the worst came from her mother."

"Her mother?"

"Yep." Conlon shook his head. "It's pretty sad, but her mother was so ashamed of Kathleen that she kept her hidden away from the world. Kathleen wasn't allowed to go to school with the other kids or do anything they did. Church was the only function she could attend outside the house, and then she had to wear a veil. It's no wonder she's afraid to let people see her face."

"I don't understand a mother who would do that to her own child." Anger coursed through Quinn. His horse danced sideways.

"Glory says in some perverted way, Kathleen's mother thought she was protecting her from further harm." He shrugged. "That's in the past. I'd like to see Kathleen become comfortable with her looks. It will take time and patience."

"I intend to have plenty of those." Quinn grinned and urged his horse to a faster walk. All this talk about Kathleen made him long to see her. He had to continue convincing her that his beliefs wouldn't stand in the way of their relationship.

Tomorrow would be the first service with the evangelist who'd arrived two days ago. Quinn planned to check with Kathleen tonight, letting her know he would pick her up in plenty of time to make the meeting.

≈

Kathleen hummed a soft melody as her needle flew through the shiny material of the dress she was making for Mrs. Monroy. She should have this finished in time for her land-lady to wear it to the evangelist's meeting tomorrow. The steady pace of her needle matched Edith's soft breathing. A couple of hours ago, Doc Meyer had come by to check her wound. The pain from changing the dressing had been enough to make Edith faint. An angry red was beginning to surround the wound, and Doc Meyer left a powder to make a poultice twice a day for her shoulder. He also gave her lau-danum to help her sleep.

"Rest will be the best healing agent." His gravelly voice made him sound gruff, but Kathleen could see the caring underneath the stern exterior. "Don't let her move any more than she has to. We don't want to aggravate the wound."

At a light knock on the door, Kathleen set aside her sewing, lowered her veil, and opened up to see who had come. Quinn stood in the hall, freshly scrubbed and shaved. He looked so handsome, her breath caught in her throat and she couldn't speak. She brushed the gauze out of the way. Quinn held her gaze for what seemed an eternity before ges-turing to the floor beside him.

"I brought some things I believe might belong to Miss Barstow. We found these two bags of ladies' clothing. I thought she would want them right away."

"Come on in, Dep. . .Quinn. Does Mrs. Monroy know you're here?" Kathleen glanced down the hallway toward the sitting room.

"Yep, she's the one who let me in. She said Miss Barstow is

sleeping." He picked up the bags and stepped inside the room.

"Yes, Doc Meyer gave her something to help her rest. I don't know when she'll wake up." Kathleen could see the disappointment on Quinn's face. "Did you have something you wanted to talk with her about?"

"Nothing particular. Just a few more questions. I figure I can't ask too much at one time, so I'll come by every day to interview her a little. How's the wound healing?"

"Doc's worried about infection setting in. He showed me how to treat the wound." Kathleen tried to hide her uncertainty. "I've never done anything like this. I worry about hurting her instead of helping."

Quinn placed the bags at the foot of the bed. Following behind him, Kathleen wasn't prepared for him to turn around so fast. They were only inches apart. She couldn't breathe. She could see that he wanted to hold her in his arms as much as she wanted to be held. Silence stretched as taunt as a rope. The only sound in the room was Edith's steady breathing.

His hand, warm against her cheek, startled, then thrilled, Kathleen. She hadn't noticed him reaching up to touch her. Never had she felt like this about anyone. *Why now, Lord? Why Quinn?* Kathleen closed her eyes and stepped away. She couldn't let this happen. Somehow, she had to discourage him. Guilt ripped through her as she watched pain flash across his face. She didn't want to hurt him.

His hand dropped to his side. "I'm sorry. I didn't mean to offend you. For the last few hours, all I've thought about is looking at you and touching you. You are so beautiful, Kathleen, so alive."

Understanding jolted her. He'd spent the day out at the site of the attack. After viewing all that death, he needed comfort. How could she deny him that? Would it be so wrong in this instance? Kathleen ignored the check in her spirit and stepped closer to Quinn.

"I'm sorry too. I misjudged your intentions. After what you've been through today, I can see why you need a person's touch." She reached up and traced her thumb along his strong jaw. His eyelids lowered. His hands caught hold of her upper arms, drawing her to him. Like a moth drawn to a flame, Kathleen couldn't seem to stop him as he lowered his head to hers. She closed her eyes. In the back of her mind, she wondered what her first kiss would be like. Never before had she allowed herself to even dream of such a thing happening.

Quinn's lips settled over hers in a warm caress. He slid his hand around her, drawing her even closer. Time stopped. A wonderful feeling of contentment settled over Kathleen. She didn't ever want this to stop.

"Kathleen, is that deputy still in there?"

At the sound of Mrs. Monroy's voice, Kathleen jerked away as if she'd been burned. Her cheeks felt on fire. Quinn gave her a lazy smile that made her heart sing.

fifteen

Tugging his string tie to tighten it, Quinn gazed at his image in the mirror. Clean shaven, his hair a little damp from the bath, he looked ready to pick up Kathleen for the church meeting. He didn't feel ready. What he was about to do would break his parents' hearts. They'd always taught him deception was the same as lying. A sin. He hadn't thought of that word in years.

I'm not deceiving anyone. Quinn wasn't sure who he tried to convince. *Religion is important to Kathleen. She is important to me. Because of that, I can go with her to church and make this sacrifice. After all, I do believe in God. Someone had to make this world. All I'm doing by going to this church meeting is supporting the woman I care about.* Quinn stared at his reflection. He could read the guilt still present in his eyes. He turned away, grabbed his hat, and dusted off the brim. Settling it on his head, he stalked out of the room. He wouldn't allow these feelings to interfere with what he planned to do. He wasn't doing anything wrong. Wincing at the prick in his conscience, Quinn shoved the feeling deep inside where he hoped it wouldn't surface again today.

The packed meeting hall showed how much the townspeople missed regular church services. For the last three days, the evangelist had been scouring the town, encouraging everyone to come to his meetings and hear the Word of God. A buzz of excitement filled the room as men and women settled onto hard benches.

Quinn steadied Maria's elbow as they inched through the crowd to find a seat. Harriet and Kathleen followed behind.

119

Once again, Kathleen had managed to pair him up with a girl he didn't want. Maria was nice enough. So was Harriet, but neither one could hold a candle to Kathleen. At least, that was his opinion. Ed Fish and John Wasson seemed to have other ideas. The two glowered at Quinn from across the room. They must think he had orchestrated this himself, leaving them out when he knew they were interested in the new schoolteachers. They couldn't be more wrong.

Part of an empty bench showed up on the left. Quinn directed Maria down the aisle. There should be enough room for the four of them if they sat close together. He fought a smile at the thought of sitting close to Kathleen. Quinn began to urge Harriet in beside Maria. She stopped, waiting for him, a smile on her face. Kathleen was nowhere in sight.

With a groan, Quinn stepped in next to Maria and waited for Harriet to take her place on the other side of him. Ed and John would believe for sure that he had designs on their girls, even though they hadn't declared their intentions.

"Where did Kathleen go?" Quinn tried to keep his distance when he asked the question.

Harriet didn't have the same reservations. She almost rested against his arm, holding her fan in front of her face as if to hide something. "She went to help Glorianna with the babies. Conlon got stopped by some of the men outside, and Glorianna couldn't handle them alone."

How had this woman known so much, when he hadn't even realized Kathleen left them? Quinn sighed and glanced across the crowded room. He caught sight of Conlon moving down the outside aisle, then saw Glorianna seated beside Kathleen, each of them snuggling one of the twins. As Conlon reached his wife, Quinn prepared to stand and beckon to Kathleen so she would know where they were sitting. Kathleen seemed to refuse Conlon's offer to take the baby. She looked across the room at Quinn and waved. She had made her choice of with whom to sit. Because of the veil covering her face, Quinn couldn't even see if she was disappointed or happy that they were apart.

For a moment, Quinn considered getting up and leaving before the meeting started. After all, he'd come here to prove to Kathleen that they were compatible despite their different beliefs. "Well, getting up and leaving won't prove a thing to her." He mumbled the words to himself.

"Did you say something?" Harriet's shoulder touched his as she spoke. Quinn could almost feel John's gaze burning into his back. How would he ever get out of this one?

"Nothing." Quinn shook his head at her.

The hum of conversation died as the evangelist stepped up on the platform. A slight breeze from Harriet's fan slid across Quinn's face. The moving air felt good. There were too many people crowded into this closed building. Already, the warmth made Quinn want to loosen his collar. By the end of the service, this many bodies would smell worse than a pack of javelinas.

The preacher greeted the crowd, introducing himself in case some of the people hadn't met him yet. He began to speak, and Quinn shut him out, choosing to let his mind wander to other things. As a boy, he'd heard enough sermons to last him a lifetime. Of course, in those days, he hadn't listened much, either. He spent most of the time ogling the girls or daydreaming about the plans he had to leave home and become a lawman. Those plans had been fulfilled.

The crowd laughed, and Quinn glanced in Kathleen's direction. Despite her veil, he knew she watched his reaction to the message. He'd better at least try to look interested and react the same way the crowd reacted. That shouldn't be too hard. He smiled, and she faced forward once again.

"I want to spend my time talking to you folks about whom you trust." The preacher pulled out a rag and wiped it across his beaked nose. "I've found something disturbing as I've traveled across the West." He glared out at the congregation as if accusing them of a terrible crime. "People out here trust in a lot of things, but they don't trust in the Lord."

One elbow on the pulpit, the preacher pointed in Quinn's direction. "Over here I see your fine deputy. I haven't met him yet, but I've heard about how he cares for this community. After talking with folks about him, I'm sure the deputy feels responsible for your welfare. He takes that charge seriously."

Sweat dribbled down Quinn's spine. People turned to stare at him as he sat between the two schoolteachers. Why was this man singling him out?

"I'm sure you folks think you can trust this deputy to provide protection for you and your families, and you can. . .to an extent."

Jaw muscles tense, Quinn fought the anger burning inside him. Had this preacher just sullied his name and reputation?

"Then, there's this fine lieutenant over here."

All heads turned in Conlon's direction.

"The other day, he and his men performed a horrible duty. I'm sure you all know about the attack, so I won't go into that. Your community is blessed to have the cavalry here to help watch out for you. I'm sure they do their best to avoid incidents like the one that happened this past week. You can trust in them. . .to an extent."

A murmur passed over the crowd. Heads moved close together as everyone seemed to wonder at the unusual way this man made his points. Quinn glanced over at Conlon, expecting to see anger. Instead, Conlon and Glorianna both had smiles on their faces. Didn't they realize what this man had said? He might be causing the whole town to doubt their ability to protect and defend. Quinn clenched his fists, longing to leave this place before he enacted violence on the preacher.

"I'd like to look at a problem the Israelites had with their protection." The evangelist peered over the pulpit, rubbed his nose, and smiled at the crowd. "You see this problem has been around since God first revealed Himself. The Israelites, during the days of Joseph, went to live in Egypt. I'm sure you remember that story. Well, there came a time when God wanted His people to leave Egypt and trust in Him. That introduced a load of suffering." He chuckled and stepped around the pulpit. Absolute silence filled the hall.

"The Israelites liked putting their trust in the Egyptians. Those Egyptians had fancy chariots and plenty of them. They had horses that were trained for war. And their horsemen had such strength everyone marveled at them."

A baby wailed. Quinn glanced at Kathleen and saw her jiggling the infant she held, probably Andrew. He could tell from the blanket. The crying ceased.

The preacher stepped behind the pulpit again. He looked down at the Bible he'd placed there. "I'd like to read a verse from the book of Isaiah the prophet in the thirty-first chapter. 'Woe to them that go down to Egypt for help; and stay on horses, and trust in chariots, because they are many; and in horsemen, because they are very strong; but they look not unto the Holy One of Israel, neither seek the Lord!' "

Looking up, the preacher gave a moment for the words to sink in. "Isaiah says later in the chapter that the Egyptians are not gods. Their men and horses are only flesh and blood. The Israelites weren't wrong to trust in the Egyptians and their tools partially, but God says don't forget to seek Him. You folks can trust in your cavalry and your deputy. That's a good idea, because these fine people will do their best to protect you from harm.

"But they are only flesh and blood. Put your trust in the Lord, Jesus Christ, who is able to always take care of you. I tell you today, He is not flesh and blood; He is God, and He is worthy of your trust."

The rest of the evangelist's words buzzed past Quinn without him hearing them. This teaching was wrong. He knew for a fact that God did not always protect His people. He didn't always have their best interests at heart. How could this man stand up there and say these things? Gripping the side of the bench, Quinn held on to keep from jumping to his feet and shouting out the hypocrisy of the message spoken here.

At the end of the service, Quinn excused himself from Maria and Harriet. Pushing through the crowd, he approached Ed and John. The two gave him looks that would make him cringe at another time. He ignored the animosity.

"Ed, John, would you two mind escorting Miss Bolton and Miss Wakefield home?"

Surprise gave the pair a startled look. They nodded, and Quinn once again pushed off through the crowd. People were milling around, chatting about the message and how wonderful this speaker was. Quinn couldn't believe how gullible they were. No wonder the Bible called these people sheep. They couldn't even see the truth for themselves.

Several men clapped Quinn on the back in greeting. He nodded and pushed past them, working his way toward Conlon. As he arrived, Glorianna and Kathleen stepped into the aisle.

"Conlon, could you give Kathleen a ride home?" Quinn almost winced at his harsh tone.

"Why, sure." Conlon shot a surprised glance at his wife.

Quinn didn't wait to see Glorianna's or Kathleen's reactions. Once more, he set off through the gaggle of people. He wanted to mow them down to get outside and away from here. Getting free couldn't happen fast enough. Shutting out all sound and focusing on the door, Quinn plowed through the mass of townsmen, heedless of the startled glances he received. Let them wonder what his hurry was. He didn't care.

The nip of winter in the air outside chilled the sweat on Quinn's face. He searched the yard for the horse and buggy he'd brought the women in. He should have offered Ed and John the use of the buggy in case they had walked or come on horses. For a moment, he pondered going inside to see if they needed the conveyance. One glance at the crush behind him and he banished the idea.

"Deputy Kirby." Mayor Allen grabbed his hand and stopped him. Quinn cast a longing glance at the buggy waiting for him. The Mayor pumped his hand like he wanted to get well water to flow. "Good to see you here, Deputy. Mighty fine sermon today."

"Yes, Sir." Quinn tried to extract his hand. People were beginning to pour out of the building. He had to get away from here. The sense of urgency was overpowering.

"I heard about that woman you rescued from the wagon train attack. Fine piece of work. That's why we hired you."

Confused, Quinn stopped and gazed at the mayor. "But, Sir, I didn't rescue her. One of the drivers brought her to town."

"That's not the story I heard." Mayor Allen beamed. People were stopping to listen, and he continued. "I heard you carried her into Mrs. Monroy's house, and you've been there several times to check on her welfare. I'm proud to have a deputy who does his job so well."

An embarrassed flush burned Quinn's cheeks. Had the whole town been talking like this? They didn't know the real reason he went to Mrs. Monroy's so often was to see Kathleen. Yes, he wanted to hear Miss Barstow's story, but her account wasn't that important. He'd already heard the driver's story. Miss Barstow couldn't have much to add other than the reason she'd been traveling with her sister.

People crushed up against him, shoving him close to the mayor. "Sir, I'll stop by and discuss this with you tomorrow." Sunlight glinted off the shine on the top of Mayor Allen's head. Quinn pulled his hand free. He started to step away.

"You do that, young man." Mayor Allen beamed in his

direction. "I'll be looking forward to a full report from you. I want to hear how you single-handedly ran off those Indians and rescued that young woman."

Quinn stopped. His mouth fell open. A murmur ran through the people standing outside. What would they think? What stories would be passed around the town now? Gritting his teeth, Quinn strode across the yard and yanked the reins free. The horse jerked its head away from him, startled at his quick movement.

"Easy, Girl." Quinn calmed the horse, then stepped around to the side of the buggy.

Quinn felt someone touch his arm. He almost groaned aloud. Not another person thinking he was some kind of hero. Looking down, he stared in shock at Kathleen standing beside him. Through the gauze of her veil, he could make out a shadowy smile.

"Conlon and Glorianna are taking you home." He gestured at the hall. "I'm sorry; I have to leave."

"Do you have an emergency?" Her soft voice touched a chord in his heart.

"No, I just need to go."

"Then I'm going with you." Kathleen stepped around him and lifted her skirts to step into the buggy. "I came to the meeting with you, and I'll return with you."

He stared up at her as she folded her hands in her lap. Blocking her face with her hand, she lifted her veil a bit and smiled at him. "Are you coming?"

sixteen

Gripping the seat between them, Kathleen did her best to maintain her balance as the buggy raced down the street. The muscles in Quinn's jaw stood out in tense relief, a testimony to the anger he must be trying to hide. What had upset him so? She could still recall the urgent feeling that raced through her when he asked Conlon to take her home. God had spoken to her heart as if in audible words, letting her know she had to go with him. She didn't know what she was to say to Quinn, but the Lord wanted her here for a reason.

The buggy careened around a corner and raced out of town. Kathleen wasn't sure where they were going, but this wasn't the way to Mrs. Monroy's boardinghouse. Relieved that Maria and Harriet weren't with them, she clung to the rocking conveyance, praying they would stop soon and that they would be safe.

As the bank of the Santa Cruz River approached, Quinn pulled on the reins, slowing the horse. He turned off the road and guided them into a small stand of trees. Sweat coated the horse's hide. The bay tossed her head, jangling the bridle and sending a long string of saliva into the air. Kathleen thought the poor horse wasn't used to being treated this way. Quinn swung down and tied the mare where she could reach some grass.

"I still can't get used to such mild weather this late in the year." Kathleen noted the way Quinn jumped at the sound of her voice as if he'd forgotten he'd brought her. "Back home we'd have ice on the ponds—even snow—and each person would be wearing enough clothes to cover two families." She almost hated resorting to such innane conversation, but she had to break the silence between them.

The anger in Quinn's eyes eased somewhat. His forehead smoothed. Kathleen breathed a little easier. Whatever had upset him must have happened during the service. Had the preacher said something? She couldn't think what. The message had been one of the best she'd heard in a long time.

Quinn crossed to her side of the buggy and reached up to help her down. Her feet settled on the ground, but Quinn kept his hold on her longer than necessary. His eyes, more gray than blue today, gazed at her. She could almost see the pain inside and wondered anew at the cause.

Kathleen unpinned her hat and placed the veiled head covering on the buggy seat. Once more, she looked up at Quinn, wishing he'd know he could talk to her. She didn't want to appear to be hiding.

"Quinn, what's wrong?" She thought to reach up and touch his cheek as she had the night before, but the memory of the kiss they shared still startled her. If she did that again, she would seem forward and that would be the wrong impression to give.

His eyes darkened. Quinn turned toward the meandering river, his jaw tense once again. Kathleen grasped his arm, hoping he wouldn't storm off, leaving her here.

"Did the preacher say something that bothered you?"

Quinn's body jerked. She could feel his muscles tighten. His fists clenched.

"He said a lot that bothered me. In fact, he didn't say much of anything I liked. I have no idea how people could sit and listen as he insulted everyone there."

"I didn't hear him insult anyone." Kathleen tried to remember the preacher's exact words to see if there was something she'd missed. Her hand slipped from Quinn's arm as he strode over to the riverbank. Lifting her skirts to clear the brush, she followed at a slower pace.

Whirling around, Quinn faced her. Deep lines dug into his forehead. His eyes flashed. "Didn't you hear what he said about Conlon and me. We do our best to protect the people in this town, and this man comes along and kicks us in the teeth. On top of that, the people applaud him for it. I felt as if no one cared whether I do my job or not."

Shock raced through Kathleen, robbing her of speech. Quinn felt his credibility had been attacked. Being a lawman was his life, and he took his duties seriously. Now, the work he'd devoted his life to had been questioned. Even if no one else in the service this morning viewed the pastor's words that way, Quinn did. His anger covered a multitude of hurts.

"Another thing." The muscles in Quinn's jaw jumped as he spoke. "That man didn't know what he was talking about."

"Why is that?" Kathleen kept her tone soft, hoping to ease Quinn's distress.

"He said that God would protect us when we needed protecting." Quinn started to rake a hand through his hair and knocked his hat to the ground. He picked the hat up and banged it against his leg. "That was a lie. I know for a fact God doesn't protect those who love Him. He allows all sorts of bad things to happen to them, and no one ever knows the reason. It's as if He can do whatever He wants and we, insignificant as we are, aren't to question Him."

Oh, Lord, how do I answer all these years of hurt and anger that he's allowed to build up? I feel You are speaking to Quinn's spirit. Otherwise, he wouldn't be so angry over this message. Please, give me the words to answer him. Help me to reach out in the right way. Kathleen waited for God to give her the wisdom to speak, but nothing came. She could only watch as Quinn turned away and stared across the river to the fields beyond.

Stepping up beside him, Kathleen took Quinn's hand in hers. This might be a bold move, but she knew he needed someone right now. If he wanted to talk, she would listen. If he wanted to stand quiet and be angry, she would stand with him and pray. Until God gave her the words, she would be silent and wait.

Long moments passed in silence. When Kathleen was almost ready to concede nothing would happen, Quinn began to speak. She held still in order to catch his quiet words. He told her the story of his sister, how she'd been different, but everyone learned to accept her as she was. Then, the new family moved in. The torment began. Bitterness made Quinn's voice harsh as he told her the story of Rupert Magee and his own part in saving Elizabeth from the bully.

"So you see, my sister loved God. My parents loved God. At that time I thought I loved God." His mouth twisted in a grimace. "All that love didn't help her at all. God refused to protect her."

"Did the boy hurt her permanently?"

"No, the bruises and cuts would heal. She could even get over the cruel taunts." Quinn's hand gripped hers so hard her fingers were going numb. He looked down at her and cupped her chin with his other hand. He stared with an intensity that was hard to face. "Don't you see? A God who protects His people should always be there for them. How would I look if I allowed bad things to happen one time and not the other? I wouldn't be a very good deputy, and I would lose my job." He shook his head. "Well, that's what happened to God. As far as I'm concerned, He lost His job."

Tears burned in Kathleen's eyes. She lowered her lids to try to hide them. How she wanted Quinn to believe in Jesus. He needed the comfort of a Savior now more than ever. A wave of compassion washed over her. All these years, Quinn hid his love for God behind indifference and anger. His hurt now was because he truly wanted to trust God, but felt he couldn't.

"Quinn, maybe you should talk to the preacher. Tell him

why you disagree with him." Kathleen refused to release his arm as he tried to turn away. "Quinn, if you were doing your job and someone disagreed with what you'd done, would you want them to be angry at you or come to you for an explanation of why you acted in the manner you did?" Afraid to even breathe, Kathleen waited to see if Quinn would understand the analogy.

Emotions played across his face like clouds across a sky on a windy day. When his eyes met hers again, she could see understanding and a sort of peace. He ran his thumb across the reddish-brown star. Her heart began to pound. She thought he might try to kiss her again. She didn't know whether to lean toward him or back away.

"Thank you." He smiled and the air warmed between them.

Her heart pounded. "What are you thanking me for?"

"For this." He stroked her bare cheek again with his thumb. "For caring enough to come with me when I was so angry. For reminding me of the right thing to do." He pulled her close and rested his cheek on the top of her head. "I'll go talk to the preacher. I don't expect anything to come of it, but I'll give him a chance to explain."

Kathleen drew away. "I'd better get home. I need to check on Edith. We all left her alone while we went to church. She'll need someone there soon to tend her needs."

"Do you think she's strong enough for me to talk with her?" The serious expression of a lawman changed Quinn's demeanor. "I'd still like to ask her some questions about her sister and herself. Maybe I can find out if she wants me to notify anyone of her sister's death."

Sadness tugged at Kathleen. "She's taking the news hard. I think even though she knew her sister probably died in the attack, she still held out a hope you would bring her back alive when you and Conlon rode out to the site. She says she has a black dress for mourning in her things, and I promised to help her change this afternoon."

Quinn slipped a hand under her elbow to steady her on the uneven path. The horse lifted its head and nickered at their approach. "I think she wants to get to the stable for her oats." Quinn helped Kathleen climb into the buggy. "I'm afraid she'll be disappointed to find out she isn't going straight home."

On the ride to town, Kathleen didn't have to hang on tight. The slower pace and the closeness to Quinn made a heady combination. She didn't want the ride to end even though she knew they had no chance together. That small, rebellious part inside her longed for a relationship with Quinn, marriage, and a family of her own. No matter how hard she tried to rid herself of those desires, they were buried deep and would come to the surface at all of the wrong times.

Now was one of those times. She could picture Quinn with a son or a daughter. Pride would shine from him. He would make a good father. Even now, he took the time to talk to them and play with Andrew and Angelina. Unlike many unmarried men, he wasn't afraid of holding the small babies. Kathleen sighed at the picture her thoughts made and pushed the impossible dreams away.

The boardinghouse echoed when they walked inside. As they drove into town, they'd seen Maria and Harriet walking down the street with Ed and John. They were going to Señora Arvizu's for supper. The foursome looked like they belonged together. Quinn had shot Kathleen a warning look as if to let her know she couldn't set him up with either of them again.

Mrs. Monroy had informed all the girls before church that she would be going to a friend's house after the service. She wouldn't be home until after the evening meal, so they would have to find something to eat themselves.

Opening the door to Miss Barstow's room, Kathleen stuck her head in, hoping she wouldn't be waking her. Doc Meyer insisted Edith needed a lot of rest from all her blood loss. When Kathleen peered around, Edith rolled over to look at her. Her swollen, red eyes told of the crying she'd been doing.

"Edith?" Kathleen slipped into the room, blocking the door so Quinn would have to wait until she had permission to let him in. "The deputy is here to talk to you. Do you think you can manage?"

"Could I wash a little first?" Edith wiped at her eyes with a hanky.

Kathleen relayed the message to Quinn, then slipped in to help Edith. By the time Quinn entered the room, Edith had pillows behind her to help her sit up a little, her face was washed, and her hair combed. She hadn't tried to cover the scar on her cheek, although she did turn her head to the side, as if to hide the blemish from them.

Amazed, Kathleen listened as Quinn questioned Edith in such a gentle manner that she didn't get very upset. He answered her questions, her main concern being that her sister hadn't been tortured or suffered, but had died quickly.

"Do you mind telling me why you and your sister were traveling to Tucson with a bunch of freight wagons rather than waiting for the stage?" The chair Quinn sat in creaked as he moved.

Picking at the blankets covering her, Edith avoided his gaze. Her face paled even further, causing the scar to stand out like a jagged bolt of lightning on a dark night.

"Is there someone you'd like me to notify? Your parents?" At Quinn's gentle question, Edith's eyes widened in horror.

"No." She tried to sit up, cried out in pain, and dropped onto the pillow. "No. He'll kill me if he finds out. Don't tell anyone."

seventeen

Clicking open Edith's valise, Kathleen glanced at the woman asleep on the bed. Edith started to move, moaned, and lay still again. She'd been so distraught after Quinn's question about notifying the family, Kathleen feared she would tear open her wound. After doing her best to calm the woman, she finally gave her some of Doc Meyer's medication to help her sleep. Then she shooed Quinn out of the house and sat by Edith's bed, assuring her everything would be fine, praying she told the truth.

Once again questions raced through her mind. Who was the man who would be angry enough to kill Edith if he found out what happened? Had her sister been a favorite and their father would be so grief stricken, he would resort to violence even though the girl's death hadn't been Edith's fault? What comfort could she offer Edith? Prayer came to mind, so she petitioned God while Edith sank into a fitful sleep.

Earlier in the day, Kathleen had talked to Edith about unpacking her bag. After all, Edith would be staying here until she gained enough strength to look for another place. She might even want to rent a room at Mrs. Monroy's. A young woman living alone could cause talk, and Kathleen knew Edith would do best to avoid that. Already rumors were flying about town since the Barstow sisters were traveling with a group of teamsters.

Kathleen laid the things from the valise on the dresser top, deciding which items to put where. Miss Barstow certainly had been traveling light. When asked where their trunks of clothes were, she'd said they had none. All they carried were

134

the two satchels and the dresses they wore. Kathleen wondered if perhaps other belongings would be sent as soon as
Edith notified someone where to ship them.

In the bottom of the bag a black dress lay folded with a
black veil beside the dress. Pulling them out, Kathleen noted
the dress seemed a little more worn than the other things in
the valise. Had Edith experienced another death in the family
recently? Was that why she seemed unusually distraught
right now? She shook her head and sighed. If one of her sisters died in such a horrible manner, she would be just as
upset as Edith—maybe more so.

With the clothes put away, Kathleen took the empty valise
and set it on the floor to push under the bed. Letting go too
soon, she noticed a thump as the bag landed. She frowned. If
the bag were empty, where did the noise come from? After
picking up the valise, she snapped the catch open and peered
inside, wondering if she'd missed a shoe or something.
Empty space greeted her.

Reaching in, she ran her hand along the bottom to see if
she could feel anything. Her fingers ran across the hidden
catch twice before she realized what the lump was. Starting
to ease the catch open, Kathleen halted. Edith had agreed for
her to unpack the bag, but would she agree to this? *Maybe
there's something in here that can help me understand why
Edith is so afraid.* Kathleen ignored the twinge of guilt that
said she was only being nosy, not helpful.

Easing open the false bottom, Kathleen could see a rather
large beaded bag and a pistol nestled together. She lifted the
expensive-looking bag from the valise. The black beads
shone in the lamplight. For some reason Kathleen shivered
as she gazed at them. Her fingers closed over the object
in the purse. She frowned. Why would Edith have this in
her bag?

Edith stirred and moaned. Kathleen jumped. Heart pounding,

she watched as Edith plucked at the covers, then lay still again. Her breathing evened out once more. A sigh of relief escaped Kathleen. She shoved the beaded bag into the valise and shut the hidden compartment. Determined not to snoop any more, she pushed the bag under the bed. With quiet steps she moved to the chair by the lamp where her sewing waited and sat down. Picking up the dress and her needle, she couldn't keep her thoughts from the object in the beaded bag.

The door to the telegraph office slammed shut after Quinn. He paid little attention as he thought of the message he'd sent across the wires. Something about Edith struck him wrong. Why would she get so upset about her family being notified of her sister's death? So far, she hadn't even told anyone much of anything about her sister. Yes, she'd cried knowing Cassie died in the attack, but she also seemed to be hiding something or from someone. The lawman in him couldn't let that go. He had to make some inquiries about Edith and see if he could figure out who she was.

Striding down the street, Quinn found himself thinking as he had all day about the message he'd heard at the church yesterday. For the hundredth time he chastised himself for reacting the way he had. Here he'd planned to show Kathleen how compatible they were, and the first chance he got, he'd blown up over a sermon that shouldn't have mattered. He didn't care about that stuff anymore. He didn't believe it, either.

This morning, when he'd stopped by to see how Miss Barstow was doing, Kathleen assured him she was resting peacefully. Before he left, she pressed a bundle of folded papers into his hand.

"I copied these scriptures, Quinn. They've helped me in tough times. Please take the time to read them and think about them. I know you're angry with God, but I'd still like you to talk to the preacher."

"I'm planning to see him today sometime." Quinn backed toward the door. "I have a lot to do, but if I can find him, I'll ask him some questions."

He'd run like a scared rabbit, folding the thick sheaf of papers and shoving them in his vest pocket. Later, he'd take the time to read what she'd written.

Touching his pocket, Quinn felt the bulge where the papers rested. He still hadn't looked at them. Even though Kathleen had given them to him, he still didn't want to be pushed. From the look of the writing on the paper, he guessed she'd copied whole passages from the Bible. His father used to carry Scripture with him, memorizing and quoting what God said, but that hadn't helped his sister, either.

Making his way down the street to the jail, Quinn ignored the activity around him. Why did everyone think they had the right to tell him how and what to believe? Every time he and Conlon were together, the man had to get in some remark about God and how Quinn should believe in Him. Kathleen didn't preach at him, but he knew she held back because of his lack of faith. She said she would never marry because of her birthmark, but he could see the longing in her eyes when she held one of the twins. If any woman deserved a husband and a family, Kathleen did. Quinn determined that somehow he would find a way to overcome their differences and become her husband.

Shaking the ring of keys, he located the one to unlock the door of the jail when he stopped. This wasn't right. His stomach couldn't take any more of this indecision. He had to prove to Kathleen that he was right when he said God would not protect His people. She wouldn't believe him, but if he could convince the preacher to talk to her, then she would have to concede the point. Most of the time, God just left His people at the mercy of whatever happenstance came along.

He didn't really care, and Quinn knew it.

Shoving the keys into his pocket, he headed down the street to the home where the evangelist stayed. Several of the families in the area had offered to put him up during the weeks he would be in Tucson. Quinn couldn't imagine wanting to have someone in your house who might start preaching at any moment.

Mrs. Dooley smiled a welcome as she opened the front door. A toddler clung to her skirts, eyes peeping out at Quinn as if he might be some monster from the dark.

"Hello, Deputy Kirby. What can I do fer you today?" Mrs. Dooley's smile displayed a tooth chipped off at an angle, the rest yellowed and stained.

"Mrs. Dooley, did I hear that the evangelist is staying with you this week?"

She beamed as if this fact made her the most important person in town. "Why, yes, he is."

"Do you think I could speak with him?" Quinn wanted to turn and run. "If he's too busy, I'll talk to him later."

"He's out back. That man sure is a worker. He's repaired my porch and fixed the fence around my chicken pen. We won't have any coyotes stealing chickens for awhile." She shuffled aside, gesturing for Quinn to come inside.

"That's okay, Mrs. Dooley. It sounds like he's a busy man. I'll come by another time."

"Oh, no, you don't. That man needs a break. I just made him sit down for a drink. You join him, and he'll rest a little longer. He doesn't have enough meat on his bones to be working so hard." The toddler peeked out again with his finger in his nose.

Taking his hat off, Quinn stepped in the house. Mrs. Dooley swept the child up into her arms, pulling his finger out of his nose. Quinn followed her to the door leading outside. There in the shade sat the preacher, his thin frame resting against the wall of the house, his eyes closed as if he were asleep.

Before Quinn could stop her, Mrs. Dooley called out, "Reverend, you've got company."

The man smiled and quirked open one eye. His eyebrow rose as if asking who would be visiting him in a town where he knew almost no one. With one fluid motion, he rose from the chair belying the ungainliness his tall, lanky body displayed.

He held out his hand to Quinn. "Name's Reilly, Son, Matthew Reilly."

Quinn took hold of his hand, surprised at the strength. "Deputy Quinn Kirby, Sir. I, uh, just stopped by to welcome you to town. I haven't had the chance to do that yet. I didn't mean to disturb your rest."

Matthew Reilly laughed as if he'd never heard anything so funny. "My rest will be when I get to heaven and live with my Lord, Son. Right now, I take a moment to sit down and pray once in awhile. Otherwise, work is the best medicine. Idle hands are a tool of the devil, you know."

Quinn nodded as if he knew exactly what the man meant. He sidled toward the corner of the house. Coming here had been a mistake. He had to leave before the conversation went further.

"Here you go, Deputy." Mrs. Dooley came out with a cup of coffee and a pot to refill the preacher's cup. "Now, you two just sit and visit awhile. I've got to run out and do some errands."

"Thank you, Ma'am." Preacher Reilly flashed her a wide smile. As the door closed behind her, he motioned to a chair beside the one he'd been resting in and sat down. Not seeing any way out, Quinn perched on the edge of the chair, his coffee warming his hands.

"I believe you were at the meeting last Sunday. Am I right?" Reilly had dark green eyes that seemed to see right into Quinn's soul.

"Yes, Sir, I was there." Quinn took a long swig of coffee and grimaced as he burnt his tongue.

"You weren't real happy with what I said."

Trying to hide his surprise, Quinn searched for the words to say. "I, uh, it's been a long time since I've been in church."

Reilly nodded. "I've had a lot of experience watching the faces of people I preach to. Some people don't listen; some thrive on the words I speak, and others get angry like you did. I admire a man who's not afraid to face what makes him mad. Now, if you don't mind, I'd like to hear what I said that you objected to."

His mind scrabbling, Quinn tried to think of a way to get out of this. Why had he come here? Who was he to try to tell this man he was wrong? Then he remembered his sister, what she'd gone through, and he could feel the anger rising up all over again. The anger and bitterness of years of hating God for what happened to his innocent sister poured out. Matthew Reilly sat silent as Quinn told the whole story, including his accusations that God didn't care what happened to the people who loved Him.

The shadows were growing long when Quinn finished talking. He couldn't look at the preacher. His eyes would be full of condemnation at Quinn's charges against God. Even knowing this, Quinn couldn't bring himself to rise and slink away like the whipped dog he felt he resembled.

"Tell me, Son, how would your sister have felt if your father refused to let her go anywhere because something bad might happen to her? In fact, what if your father made you stay at home and never let you decide anything you wanted to do whether right or wrong?"

"My father wouldn't have done that." Quinn looked at Reilly in surprise. "He loved us too much to treat us in that manner."

A faint smile lit the preacher's eyes. "That's a good father, then, wouldn't you say?"

Quinn nodded. "He was always a good father. He guided us, but he also let us make some mistakes."

Reilly's dark green eyes gazed at the sky as a few clouds scudded past. "You see, Son, that's sort of the way God did things too."

Quinn blinked in surprise.

"When God made the garden for Adam and Eve, He made it a perfect place. Every day He came down and talked with Adam and Eve. He wanted them to do right always, but He wanted the choice to be theirs. You know what happened?"

A lump filled Quinn's throat. He nodded.

"They committed the first sin." Reilly rubbed his chin. "Seems to me we've been doing that ever since. You see, God didn't want us to be like the animals. The Bible says He wants us to fellowship with Him. Do you know why He allows us to make our mistakes?"

Tightness wrapped around Quinn. He felt like he couldn't get a breath.

"Because He loves us so much." Reilly's eyes were serious. "Just like your daddy let you and your sister make choices that weren't always right, God lets each one of us make our own decisions. You see, some people make pretty poor choices and everyone suffers for that."

"But, why didn't God step in and protect my sister?" The tightness almost made speaking impossible for Quinn.

"How do you know He didn't?"

"She got hit with a rock and hurt pretty bad."

"Maybe that rock should have hit her hard enough to kill her." The preacher sat forward and clasped his hands over his knees as if in prayer. "You see, we can't know the mind of God. Who's to say how much He protected Elizabeth?"

Stumbling up from his chair, Quinn mumbled something. He set his coffee cup on the porch railing, then almost ran around the house to leave. He couldn't stay longer. This couldn't be right. Had he been wrong all these years? Had he misunderstood what God had done? Half running down the street, all he could think of was his need to escape the thoughts careening through his head.

eighteen

Andrew gurgled and stretched a tiny hand up to Kathleen's face. He grabbed her lip and tugged.

"Ouch." Kathleen loosened his fingers one by one as Andrew gave her a toothless smile. "You are so proud of yourself." She tried to act angry at the fat baby. "I'll have to get you now." She lifted him and nibbled his neck, causing him to give off infectious chuckles that soon had them both laughing.

"Are you spoiling that boy again?"

Kathleen jumped. Andrew started, his face puckering as if he were about to cry. "Oh, don't you cry, Sweetie. Your mommy just scared me, that's all." She frowned at Glorianna. "Next time don't sneak up on us. I could have dropped him."

Putting Angelina on the rug in the middle of the room, Glorianna grinned. "A team of horses in a full gallop could have sneaked up on you two, you were laughing so loud." She reached for Andrew, gave him a kiss on the cheek, and put him down with his sister. Glorianna sank onto the settee beside Kathleen and collapsed with a sigh. "I was prepared for one baby to make me tired, but two are double the work. Some days, I don't know what I'd do without you and Alicia helping out."

Watching the two infants, Kathleen couldn't help but smile as Andrew began to look around at the various objects within his sight. Angelina did her best to follow the voices talking. "You are a very good mother, Glory. These babies are such blessings."

"You need some of your own." Glorianna put a hand on

143

Kathleen's arm. Her eyes filled with compassion.

Hurt and anger swept through Kathleen. She stiffened at her cousin's touch. "I can't marry, Glorianna, and you know that."

"Can't or won't?" Fire sparked in Glory's eyes.

"Can't." Kathleen tried to hold onto her resolve in the face of Glory's determination. She'd never been able to win an argument with Glory.

"I am getting tired of listening to you feel sorry for yourself because of a little mark on your cheek." Angelina and Andrew both looked their direction as their mother's tone became firm. "You always lectured me about not being afraid to step out and be what God wants me to be. If that's true, then why are you still hiding behind that veil? Why can't you believe God made you as you are, and to Him and to those who know you, you're beautiful?"

Angelina whined, a sure sign she was getting ready to cry. Glorianna ignored her and took Kathleen's hands. "You're going to ruin God's plans for you by not allowing Him to work." Glory's eyes filled with tears. "Take off that mask, Kathleen. Quit shutting yourself away from everyone. Allow people the chance to love you as much as I do. Let God know you trust Him to protect you, no matter what."

The words felt like physical blows that battered Kathleen from one side, then the other. She tried to fight down a surge of anger. "You have no idea what my life has been like. How can you expect me to live like that?"

"Do you think you're the only one ever to be made fun of? Imagine how I felt, moving around so much with Daddy in the cavalry. I was always the new girl." Glory's eyes narrowed for a moment. "I can't tell you how many people have asked about you since you arrived. They care, Kathleen. They aren't children. Why can't you give them a chance?" Glory's fingers dug into Kathleen's arm.

Jumping to her feet and rushing for the door, Kathleen

almost fell over Angelina. The baby began to wail. Glorianna reached for her daughter as Kathleen backed away, groping for her hat and veil.

"I have to go." Kathleen choked out the words as she turned toward the door.

"Wait." Glory's voice halted her in midstep. "Kathleen, you were so brave to come all the way out here like you did. All your life, your mother kept you shut away from the world. Your only real memories are those of cruel taunts you suffered as a child. Trust God. He's done a good work in you, and He's longing to do more."

After stumbling off the porch, Kathleen made her way down the path to the street. Tears blinded her even worse than the blackness of the veil over her eyes. What would happen if she were to rip this gauze off? She shuddered. Horror crept up her spine, sending chills racing down her arms. Glory didn't understand. She'd never been made fun of to the extent Kathleen had. No one could understand that unless they'd been through the same.

A picture of the Bible description of Jesus at the mercy of the soldiers who arrested Him flashed through her mind. She gasped. Last night she'd read that very story in her Bible time. Jesus had done nothing wrong. He was perfect, yet they spit on Him, mocked Him, and called Him names. What they did to Jesus was far worse than anything anyone had ever done to her. What had He done to them? He'd asked forgiveness for the very ones who abused Him.

Going around to the back of Mrs. Monroy's house, Kathleen took out the key to her sewing room. Her hand shaking, she missed the lock twice before the key slipped home and turned. The door swung open. Kathleen fell through, her hand covering her mouth to hold in the sobs. *Oh, God, have I been disobedient? Have I been hiding and not trusting You to protect me? Lord, I know how You suffered, but*

I feel so alone and unable to face something like that. Help me.

Kathleen ran to her room, fell to her knees, and rested her forehead against the bed. For a long time she stayed there, resting in the touch of her Savior's hand as He comforted her. When she stood, she removed the veil from her hat. Walking to where she kept her scraps of cloth, she threw the bit of fabric into the discard pile.

"Jesus, thank You for helping me to forgive. Now, help me to have the courage to walk out of here like this." Kathleen closed her eyes. "This is the way You made me, Lord. Help me to rejoice and be glad." Lightness filled her. She felt as if she could float on the clouds. Laughter bubbled up, escaping into the room. She hadn't realized how heavy her burden had been until she gave her fears to the Lord. Tears of joy streamed down her cheeks.

"Kathleen, are you in there?" A knock sounded from her bedroom door. Mrs. Monroy called out to her. Wiping the wetness from her cheeks, Kathleen hurried to open the door. Mrs. Monroy started to speak, then stopped with her mouth open. She stared at Kathleen.

"Why, young lady, you are a beauty. Why have you been hiding under that veil?" She took hold of Kathleen's chin and turned her face. As the birthmark came into view, her expression softened. "Look at that." Her hand covered the star on Kathleen's cheek. "When I was a girl, our neighbor had something like this. My mother used to call it an angel's kiss. That's no reason to hide, Honey. I hope you know that."

Her throat ached. Kathleen managed to nod. "I understand now."

Mrs. Monroy straightened. "I want you to speak with Miss Barstow. Something is wrong with that woman."

"What's happened?" Kathleen started to reach for her hat and veil before she remembered. She took Mrs. Monroy's arm and led her out the door.

"She's become like a different person. I came to her room after lunch to find her up and getting dressed. She says she's got work to do. I ask you, what kind of work can a woman do when she has a gunshot wound in her shoulder? When I told her to get back in bed, she gave me such a cold look I near froze to death."

"That doesn't sound like Edith." Puzzled, Kathleen hurried to the injured woman's room, Mrs. Monroy huffing along behind her. Giving a light knock, she opened the door and peeked in. "Edith, may I come in?"

"I can't stop you." The cold voice sounded so different from the near invalid Kathleen had stayed with for days. Then she'd been quiet, acquiescent, so withdrawn Kathleen had wondered if she would ever recover. Now, she sounded almost brassy, defiant—a different person than the one who'd been in this room previously.

Miss Barstow stood before a small mirror, trying to pin up her hair with one hand. The lush, brown waves were not cooperating. Several pieces of hair straggled down around her face. As if exasperated, Edith started to lift her injured arm to do the job two-handed. A grimace of pain crossed her face. She dropped the brush, which fell to the floor with a sharp crack.

"I'll leave you to see what you can do," Mrs. Monroy whispered behind Kathleen. Her heavy tread receded down the hall.

"Let me help you with your hair." Kathleen stepped in and shut the door. "I don't know how I could do mine with one hand."

Edith yanked out the pins she'd already used, sending her hair cascading to her waist. Glancing around, she caught sight of Kathleen and turned, her eyes wide. Kathleen's hand itched to cover her cheek. She smiled at Edith.

"I hope your brush isn't hurt."

"I'm sure it's fine." Edith continued to stare. Kathleen picked up the brush and, as she stood, Edith stretched out her hand to touch Kathleen's face. "Is this why you always wore the veil?"

Kathleen nodded.

Placing a hand over her jagged scar, Edith seemed to lose her anger. "I'm sorry I spoke harshly with you. You've been so kind to me. Thank you."

"Where are you going?" Kathleen glanced around the room. "I see you have your bags packed."

Edith turned. Her brown hair looked pale over the black of her dress. "I need to get something from town, then I'll be leaving."

"I thought you planned to live here."

"That's before my sister died." Edith's shoulders sagged as if a great weight sat on them. "I want to return home. There's some unfinished business I have to attend to."

"Can I help you with anything?" Kathleen longed to put her arms around Edith. She seemed so alone in the world.

"If you'd help me with my hair, I would appreciate it." Edith sat in a chair so Kathleen could do the chore. Tension seemed to radiate out from her as Kathleen brushed her hair, then pinned it up. The waves were so becoming. Edith turned and smiled her thanks. Picking up her hat and veil, she paused at the door. Her light eyes hardened, all compassion gone.

"I know you care for that deputy. You might want to go visit him and keep him company."

Before Kathleen could respond, Edith pinned the hat in place and disappeared out the door. What had she meant about Quinn? Had he been here today looking for her? The thought of seeing him set her blood racing, but having the courage to walk down the streets in the open proved daunting. Instead, she returned to her rooms and organized her sewing, rearranging items that didn't need it.

Sinking onto a chair, she buried her head in her hands. "I'm so sorry, Lord. Just this afternoon I promised to have courage and trust in Your protection. Mrs. Monroy and Edith were both so kind. There's nothing for me to be afraid of, but I'm scared. Will You take my hand and walk with me to see Quinn?"

Taking a deep breath, Kathleen stood, walked out the door, and locked it behind her. For some reason, Edith's comment about Quinn bothered her, but she couldn't decide why. Her steps quickened, an urgency building inside. Beside her she felt a comforting presence as if the Lord walked there, lending her His courage.

≈

Rubbing a hand over his unshaven jaw, Quinn winced at the raspy sound. His vest hung open, his shirt wrinkled. Even his badge appeared tarnished and off center. He felt as if he were falling apart and didn't know which way to turn. All night long, he'd wrestled with the questions raised by the preacher, but the answer he sought seemed as distant as ever. Walking the streets last evening to keep tabs on the action in town, he'd been surly to at least a dozen people. He would have to look them up and apologize, but right now the retraction would be worse than the offense.

Touching the side of his vest, Quinn thought of the Scriptures Kathleen had given him. She said they were verses she'd memorized and that they'd helped her. Some of the papers were worn; others looked as if they'd only been copied in recent days. Off and on during the night, he'd read from the verses, thought on the preacher's conversation and sermon, and argued aloud that this wasn't true. God didn't care about anyone. Somehow, he'd been unable to convince himself. If what he believed was true, then why were so many of the people he admired adamant about their belief in God's protection?

Pounding hooves raced down the street outside the office. Quinn grabbed his hat and surged to his feet. Whoever was on that horse was traveling too fast. He tugged at his vest, too much in a hurry to straighten his clothes anymore. Before he could reach for the handle, the door burst open. Paulo Rodriquez fell to the floor, springing up again with the agility of youth.

"*Señor, andele, por favor.*" He turned to rush out the door. Quinn caught hold of the boy's shirt and hauled him back.

"Whoa, Paulo, speak slow and in English." Paulo panted, his open mouth dragging in great gulps of air. His black eyes were wide with fear. "Sorry, Señor. You must hurry, please."

"What's the problem?"

Paulo danced from foot to foot. "She's here. Come on." He took Quinn's hand and tugged so hard Quinn almost lost his balance.

"Who's here, Paulo?" Last night's lack of sleep made Quinn want to grab the boy and shake him until his teeth rattled. Taking a deep breath, he stooped and looked Paulo in the eye, trying to help the boy calm down.

"The lady, Señor deputy. She's here, and she has a gun. You have to come."

Quinn frowned. A lady with a gun? Most women didn't carry guns.

"What lady and what is she doing with the gun?"

Paulo's eyes filled with tears. "The lady in black. She has her face covered. She wants much money."

The lady in black? Face covered? A veil! Quinn snapped up, his brain struggling to register the information. He'd been so distraught over talking with the preacher, he hadn't met the stage yesterday evening. Had the Veiled Widow come to town on the stage the one day he missed being there? That couldn't be. Grabbing Paulo's shoulders, Quinn tried to get control of himself. He could see the fear in the boy's eyes and knew he was the cause now.

Easing his grip, he tried speak calmly. "Paulo, tell me where the woman is. Who is she pointing the gun at?"

"At the offices of Lord and Williams, Señor. She says they owe her, and she wants money and two horses. I was there with my papa. He helped me sneak out the door so I could come and get you. Please, Señor, hurry."

"Paulo, I want you to go home. I'll take your horse, but I don't want you to follow me. Understand?"

Paulo nodded, and Quinn headed for the door. As he raced for the horse, he checked the pistol strapped to his side. He had to stop this woman before she killed someone.

nineteen

A small body hurtled into Kathleen's as she rounded the corner of the street leading to the jail. Her breath whooshed out. She grabbed the person, trying to keep both of them from falling.

"Paulo, what are you doing?" Kathleen gasped. Her stomach ached from the hit.

Big, black eyes gazed at her with terror. He didn't recognize her without her veil. She'd seen him a few times with his mother at Glory's house, but she'd always been careful to keep the covering in place when they were around.

"Paulo, it's okay. I'm Kathleen, Glorianna's cousin. I usually have a veil on. Remember?"

He nodded, his brow furrowed as if he recognized the voice, but not the face. His small chest heaved, out of breath from his headlong dash. His eyes still held a look of fear, but she didn't believe she was the cause anymore.

"He said I have to go right home." Paulo hopped to one side. She kept her hold on his arms.

"Your father sent you home?"

"No, the deputy. He said I shouldn't follow him, but I should go home." Paulo glanced behind him as if Quinn would be watching and know he wasn't hurrying home.

"Have you been bothering Deputy Kirby?" Kathleen couldn't figure out why Quinn had been so harsh with the boy. Paulo loved to talk with Quinn, and Quinn enjoyed the boy too.

Paulo whispered, as if imparting a confidence. "He's going to shoot her, and he doesn't want me to see."

152

Kathleen could feel the color drain from her face. "Who's he going to shoot?" Paulo's brow knit as her grip tightened on his arms. She forced herself to relax.

"The lady in black." Paulo glanced behind him once more. "She is going to shoot someone at the office of Lord and Williams. I told Deputy Kirby, and he will shoot her and save my papa."

The woman in black. Kathleen recalled all the times Quinn referred to this criminal and how he arrested her, thinking she was the Veiled Widow. Fear wrapped around her as she thought of Quinn facing this danger.

"Paulo, I want you to go on home." She released the boy. He hesitated.

"Don't go where the black lady is. She scares me. She talks like a *bruja*, a witch." His black eyes widened. He looked terrified.

"Don't worry about me, Paulo. You go on home to your mama."

The boy raced past her. She knew she should watch to make sure he continued on home, but the urgency to get to Quinn made her gather her skirts and race off in the opposite direction. Heart-pounding scenarios began racing through her mind as she hurried down the empty roadway. Pictures of Quinn lying still and pale with blood on his shirt made her pray harder than she ever had before.

The buildings she sought came into view. The street was deserted except for a few horses tied at hitching posts. An ominous quiet huddled over the town. Kathleen slowed her headlong pace, trying to catch her breath. Heedless of the danger, she pushed through the doors into the offices of the Lord and Williams building.

A slender woman in black faced Quinn. His back was to the door, but Kathleen could read the tension in the set of his shoulders as he trained his pistol on the woman. As Kathleen rushed in, the woman glanced at the door. She took a step closer to the rear door. Quinn didn't move, his gaze never wavering from the woman, his gun not faltering.

Time seemed to slow. Kathleen noted several things at once. A black beaded bag dangled from the woman's wrist; she held a pistol pointed at Quinn; several men cowered in one corner of the office, and a lock of wavy, light brown hair hung loose on the woman's shoulder. Kathleen gasped.

"I'm telling you for the last time, Widow, put the pistol down."

The woman's head turned from side to side as if she were looking between Quinn and Kathleen. The barrel of the pistol wavered, then lowered. The thump of the pistol hitting the floor echoed in the silent office. The woman's shoulders sagged. She took another step.

"Quinn." Kathleen had to tell him.

His head whipped around for an instant. "Kathleen, get out of here."

The woman moved again as Quinn's attention left her. Kathleen could feel the stares of the men in the room. Her hand brushed her cheek as she remembered she wasn't wearing her veil. *Lord, help me.* A surge of peace settled over her.

"Stop." Quinn's command halted everyone. The veiled woman froze in midstep. "You aren't sneaking out of here. I've waited and watched for you. . .and now you're coming to jail with me."

Somehow, the woman had slipped her hand in the bag dangling from her wrist. Panic began to overwhelm Kathleen. She had to stop this.

"Quinn, you've got to listen."

"Kathleen, get out of here now." Anger infused Quinn's voice.

The woman took another step as if she thought Quinn too distracted to notice. Any minute, she would be close enough to dash through the door and attempt an escape. The shot from Quinn's gun startled Kathleen. The Veiled Widow jumped, then raised her beaded bag.

"No, Edith." Kathleen tried to rush forward. The sound of a second shot broke the tension. Quinn stumbled. His gun bucked and the woman cried out. Quinn clutched his chest and folded over on himself, collapsing to the floor. The woman fell straight back, her small body making little noise as she hit the floor.

❧

Quinn heard the door crash open behind him. He saw the Widow start and glance in that direction. He didn't move. She had never been known to work with anyone or have an accomplice of any kind. This was probably Paulo disobeying his directive. The boy would be in trouble when this was over. Right now, Quinn refused to be distracted.

He gave the order for her to drop her gun. Shocked, he watched her obey. Events began to unfold fast. Kathleen was here. He didn't want her here. The woman he loved shouldn't be in danger. Loved? Warmth rushed through him at the thought. Would she ever be able to love him? He pulled his thoughts away from such dangerous territory and forced them to return to the matters at hand. He saw the Widow trying to make a break for the door. His finger closed over the trigger, and he shot into the floor next to her, wanting to frighten her into complying with him. He couldn't lose her after waiting so long.

She raised her hands as if she were surrendering. The black, beaded bag dangled from her left wrist. Her right hand was inside the bag. Kathleen shouted Edith's name for some reason. A blow slammed into his chest. His hand jerked up. His finger tightened on the trigger. The gun fired, then fell from his hand. He couldn't breathe. As he crumpled forward, the light in the room faded away.

Voices called his name from a distance. He heard Kathleen. Opening his mouth, Quinn tried to speak to her, but the sound wouldn't come. In the dimness he felt a presence. Peace stole over him. Was he dying? If so, he didn't seem to care. Somehow, he knew everything would be all right.

A wave of pain washed over him. His left side ached as if he'd been kicked by a mule. Booted feet clumped on the floor near his head. Hands touched him. Voices spoke, hazy, but getting clearer. The room began to come into focus.

"I think he's coming to." A man's voice spoke.

Kathleen knelt beside him. Her veil had fallen off. He'd never seen a more beautiful sight than the star-shaped mark on her cheek.

"Quinn, can you hear me?" Her beautiful lips formed the words. Fascinated with the way she spoke, he wished to stay still and watch her. She didn't seem to have the same desire. Her hand cupped his cheek. "Quinn, you were shot, but you're okay. She had a derringer in her bag. Because of the papers, the bullet only penetrated the skin. Doc Meyer already popped the lead out."

Memories of what happened flooded over him. He tried to get up. What happened to the Veiled Widow? Was she getting away?

Kathleen pushed down on him. "Quinn, stop." The sharpness of her voice halted him. "Don't worry. You shot her. She's alive, and the doc is looking at her."

"Am I hit bad?" Quinn knew with certainty he didn't want to die. He wanted a long life. A life filled with days spent with Kathleen and a family.

She smiled. "I've never seen a better example of God's protection than this." She held up a thick sheaf of folded papers. They were the scriptures she'd copied. He'd read them, folded them tightly, and put them in his inside vest pocket. He remembered thinking they were so thick folded up that they made the vest bulge out. The center of the papers held a bullet hole. The Word of God had slowed the bullet. Once more, the preacher's message came rushing back to him.

Gritting his teeth, Quinn eased up to his feet. A trickle of blood stained his shirt. He refused to consider what would have happened if her gun had been a bigger caliber or if he'd been standing closer. By tomorrow, he'd be sporting a whopper of a bruise. He could see Doc Meyer working on the woman. He took a step in that direction when Kathleen halted him.

"Quinn." She waited for him to look at her. "It's Edith—Miss Barstow."

He glanced over at Doc, then at Kathleen. Had he heard right?

"Edith is the criminal you've been looking for. I didn't figure it all out until I saw her here. Then I knew. When I put her things away, I found the guns in her valise. That's how I knew she had the little, hidden derringer. I tried to warn you."

"I don't understand. Why was she traveling with her sister?"

"No one knows." Kathleen's eyes reflected such sadness, he couldn't resist taking her hand. "If she doesn't live, we may never know."

"Your veil." Quinn brushed a finger across Kathleen's velvety cheek. "Where is it?" She smiled, and he couldn't breathe.

"Glory gave me a tongue lashing that I sorely needed. I realized I needed to trust God to protect me from mean comments. I had to quit hiding. It's been hard, but these people are wonderful." She gestured to several of the men talking in small groups at the rear of the office.

Jerking his hand away, Quinn limped across to where Doc worked on Edith. Doc gave him a grim prognosis, and Quinn stalked from the room, ignoring the hurt look on Kathleen's face. He couldn't stay longer. Every time something happened lately, he had to hear about God's protection. *God, won't You leave me alone? My life was fine, but now I don't even know which way to turn.*

࿏

A chill wind blew down the street, making Quinn wish he'd put on his jacket. Standing outside the meeting hall, he could hear the people singing. He didn't want to go inside. This was the last service before the preacher moved on. An invisible force seemed to drag him here. For several nights, he hadn't slept well. He felt like he was in the middle of a battle, and he didn't know which side would win.

Ever since Edith Barstow had died from the gunshot wound he'd accidentally inflicted on her, he'd avoided all the people he cared about. The desire to see Kathleen had become a physical ache over the days. A sense of justice kept him from seeking her out. He didn't think he could keep from asking her to marry him, yet he knew because of his lack of faith, she would say no. He couldn't bear that.

The music ended. Quiet settled over the hall. He could almost see the lanky preacher walking to the pulpit and opening his Bible. The wind gathered behind him, pushing with enough force to make him take a step. He tried to fight. His feet seemed to have a will of their own, dragging him through the door to an empty seat in the back.

"I'd like to read a scripture from the book of Jeremiah the prophet, chapter seventeen." Matthew Reilly looked over the crowd, his eyes meeting Quinn's. " 'Thus saith the Lord; Cursed be the man that trusteth in man, and maketh flesh his arm, and whose heart departeth from the Lord. For he shall be like the heath in the desert, and shall not see when good cometh; but shall inhabit the parched places in the wilderness, in a salt land and not inhabited.' "

I'm cursed, Lord. All this time I thought I was so smart

trusting in man's goodness. It wasn't true. God forgive me.
Quinn fought tears that threatened to overflow. He wanted to
run out of the building, but he couldn't seem to move.

"Now I want to read you the next part of that passage."
The preacher's voice cut in on Quinn's thoughts. " 'Blessed
is the man that trusteth in the Lord, and whose hope the Lord
is. For he shall be as a tree planted by the waters, and that
spreadeth out her roots by the river, and shall not see when
heat cometh, but her leaf shall be green; and shall not be
careful in the year of drought, neither shall cease from yield-
ing fruit.' "

Hope burned like a flame in Quinn's heart. *Lord, I want to
trust in You, not in myself, not in man. I want to believe in
Your protection. Help me, Lord. Forgive me for all these
years of doubting You.*

The service ended. Quinn heard nothing more than the
passages of scripture and the preacher asking for those to
come forward who needed prayer or salvation. As if in a
dream, Quinn made his way down the aisle.

&

Kathleen snuggled Angelina against her breast. She brushed
her cheek against the sleeping infant. The touch of soft skin
against hers never failed to amaze her. Glorianna gasped
beside her. Kathleen glanced at her cousin. Glory had tears in
her eyes. Conlon, too, had shiny eyes. Kathleen turned her
gaze to the front, where the preacher knelt praying with a
man. Quinn? Was that Quinn, the man she loved, kneeling at
the altar? Tears ran down her cheeks as she gave her thanks
to God for another miracle.

People began milling around, some making their way out.
Kathleen watched as Quinn stood, spoke to the evangelist for
a few minutes, then began to search the crowd. Her heart did
a little dance in anticipation. Quinn's eyes met hers. He
smiled, and she knew. She knew without a doubt that he

loved her as much as she loved him. She handed Angelina to Glory. As the crowd thinned and they could see one another better, Kathleen watched Quinn mouth the words that made her heart sing. "I love you."

epilogue

Gripping the side of the buggy with one hand, Kathleen stared out at the velvety, green grass and trees lining the road. Her other hand rested on the small mound of her stomach. She smiled at Quinn, reveling in the love that shone in his eyes. They'd been married six months, and she'd finally agreed to go with him to visit his family.

"Are you. . ."

"Kathleen, for the thousandth time, I'm sure my family will love you just as you are and just as much as I do." Putting his hat on the seat, he pulled the buggy to a stop and kissed her. "I think you keep asking me that just so I'll stop and kiss you." His eyes twinkled.

She could feel her face flame. "I do not." She wrinkled her nose at him. "Well, you don't seem to be complaining."

He kissed her again. "You're right; I don't." He rattled the reins, urging the horses to go. "We'll be there in about half an hour."

The sun shone with a golden warmth that felt good. Kathleen knew she would get too hot later in the day, but right now she needed to be warm. Since the day she'd stopped hiding behind her veil, she'd become so free. The people in Tucson proved wonderful. No one ever made her feel unwelcome. Glorianna said if Kathleen thanked her one more time for confronting her on that issue, she would give her the twins for a whole week. Kathleen smiled. Those twins were a handful.

Her only worry was that Quinn's family would find her lacking. He'd assured her many times they wouldn't, but she'd lived with years of doubt. Quinn even said that after they visited his folks, they would travel on to see her family. She couldn't repress a shudder. Her mother would be horrified to see her face uncovered. Quinn insisted he would set the matter straight, and somehow Kathleen knew he would.

Since the day Quinn became a Christian, he'd changed so much. Even though he hadn't admitted it to anyone, he blamed himself for Edith's death. As a lawman, he felt so responsible for everyone, even the criminals. Before she died, Edith had awakened enough to talk to Kathleen. She told her the whole story of how her father, in a drunken bout of gambling, sold her sister to a horrible man. This man forced her to do unspeakable things, often beating her for the sheer pleasure the violence brought him. Edith's father didn't care about anything other than where his next drink was coming from. Edith's mother was dead, so Edith knew that she was the only one who could rescue Cassie.

Edith had no money, and her ploy of getting cash or gold from men had begun innocently. She'd always been beautiful. The scar she'd received as a young girl seemed to add to her mystique. She preyed on the men only to get the means to help her and her sister make a new start somewhere they would never be found. Before she died, she told Kathleen where to find the remainder of the money so at least some of it could be returned. Quinn and Kathleen talked for hours about how Edith's need to protect her sister rather than turning to God for protection had brought only heartache and grief.

"Are you still with me?" Quinn's arm slipped around her shoulder.

"I'm sorry. I was thinking about Edith."

Sadness stole over Quinn's face. He pulled Kathleen close. "At least she has a chance for true happiness. After you talked to her, I believe she understood her need for Jesus. That's the best gift you could show her."

Resting her head against his shoulder, Kathleen sighed. She'd never thought she could be so content.

The buggy rounded a corner. Quinn guided the horse around a turn onto a narrow lane. Before them, a house and outbuildings sprawled against the landscape. Several horses in a corral raised their heads and whinnied. The door to the house opened, and a man stepped out. Even from this distance, Kathleen could see the resemblance to Quinn. The way he stood, then his stride as he came toward them made her wonder if she would mistake him for his son in the dark. Coming closer, she could see the strong jaw and thick blond waves of hair like Quinn's. Even his eyes seemed to be the same color of blue-gray.

Quinn pulled the buggy to a stop and hopped down. His father halted a few feet away, and the two faced each other for the first time in years. Kathleen held her breath, waiting to see what would happen.

Mr. Kirby took a long stride forward and embraced Quinn. "Welcome home, Son. It's been too long."

Tears burned in Kathleen's eyes as she watched the reunion.

"Quinn." A woman raced out the door and across the yard. Her face shone with excitement as she almost threw herself at Quinn.

"Mom." Quinn sounded choked as he hugged the small woman. Her head only reached his chest, and she looked as if a strong wind would blow her away.

"Who's this?" Quinn's father was standing by the buggy studying Kathleen.

Releasing his mother, Quinn turned to help Kathleen down. Her legs felt unsteady. Grateful for Quinn's arm around her, she leaned against him for support.

"This is my wife, Kathleen. Kathleen, my parents, James and Mary Kirby."

With a cry of joy, her mother-in-law embraced Kathleen.

Quinn's father shook his hand, then kissed Kathleen on the cheek—right on top of her star-shaped birthmark. "Welcome to the family, Kathleen."

Mary shot Quinn an accusing look. "You could have sent a letter telling us. That telegram only mentioned you coming for a visit." She grabbed Kathleen by the arm. "Let's go into the house. It sounds like we have a lot of catching up to do."

Kathleen followed her mother-in-law into the frame house. Bright rag rugs decorated polished wooden floors. A few wooden toys lay scattered in one corner of the room. Quinn and his father followed them in after watering the horse and turning the tired animal loose in the corral.

"I just finished baking a dried apple pie." Mary brought out some plates and lifted the cooling pie from the counter. "Elizabeth and her family will be here for supper. She'll be so excited to meet you, Kathleen. I can see you two have something special in common."

Quinn sat beside Kathleen and wrapped her hand in his as if he understood her discomfort. His smile and eyes spoke of his love without a word. Warmth and peace flowed through her.

"I didn't know Elizabeth married." Quinn gave his mom a puzzled look. "Why didn't you write and tell me?"

Mary gave James a glance Kathleen couldn't interpret. She seemed hesitant to answer Quinn's question.

"I don't believe you've written in awhile." James accepted his piece of pie, giving his wife a smile. "You sent the telegram saying you were coming, but that was the first we knew you were in Tucson. Your mother wrote to you at the last address we had in Colorado, but the letter came back to us with a note that they didn't know where you were."

Quinn's face reddened. He gave his parents a sheepish look. "I guess I haven't been too good about writing." He cut a bite of pie. "So, tell me about Elizabeth and her family. Who'd she marry?"

Another uneasy glance passed between his parents, but Kathleen didn't think Quinn noticed. She wondered what was wrong.

Mary began to talk in a tone that sounded contrived and unnaturally cheerful. "Elizabeth's been married over two years. She has a boy, Seth, and a new baby girl, Emily Anne. She's the sweetest little thing."

Swallowing a bite of pie, Quinn seemed to catch on to the tension in the room. "Who'd she marry?" He asked the question in a soft voice, placing his fork on the plate beside his uneaten portion of pie.

James pushed away from the table and stood. "Son, why don't you and I go outside. I'll show you some of the changes we've made to the place."

The muscles in Quinn's jaw bunched. Kathleen rested her hand on his arm and could feel the tightness there.

"Dad, you're avoiding the question. What happened to Elizabeth, and who'd she marry?"

Sinking into his chair, James rubbed his hands over his face and reached over to take Mary's hand. Her brow knit as if she were worried.

"Elizabeth is now Elizabeth Magee. She married Rupert."

"What?" Quinn surged to his feet. Kathleen caught his hand and began to pray. She hadn't seen him this distraught since before he'd become a Christian.

"How could you let her do that? Did he threaten you? Or her?" Quinn's free hand bunched into a fist. "I should have stayed to make sure she'd be safe."

James rose to his feet. Anger shone in his eyes. "Sit down." At his command, Quinn sat down, and his dad followed suit. "I want you to listen to this story before you go jumping to conclusions."

"You told me the Magees left town."

"They did. The day after you left, they packed up and moved.

There was a lot of speculation about what happened. No one around here regretted their leaving." Mary took hold of her husband's hand, and Kathleen appreciated the love between the two of them.

"Three years ago, Rupert returned by himself. His father died the previous spring." James seemed uncomfortable about going on. "I don't know how you feel about the Lord these days, Quinn. When you left home, you were dead set against believing."

Bowing his head, Kathleen thought Quinn must be remembering with regret the words spoken in haste before he left and the years following. "I turned my back on Jesus. I was hurt and angry and thought I could do everything on my own without God. Last fall, I found out different. I gave my life to Jesus—partly because of Kathleen's prayers and witness."

Mary gave a cry of joy. Tears sparkled in her eyes. She came around the table and gave Quinn a long hug. "I'm so happy, Quinn. We've prayed every single day for you."

He nodded and cleared his throat. "Thank you for that. But, I'd like to know what this has to do with Magee."

"Well, you see Rupert returned for one reason. He came to apologize to Elizabeth for the way he treated her when he lived here. Through a series of events he too became a Christian." James paused to study his son. "I have a feeling you've changed a lot in the last few months. Am I right?"

Quinn nodded. Kathleen couldn't help smiling as she thought of the considerate, caring man he'd become.

"Well, Rupert is the same way. He's no longer brash and obnoxious, demanding his way. You couldn't ask for a better husband for your sister. He treats her like a princess, and he loves those kids in a way most fathers never do."

Kathleen could almost see the thoughts turning in Quinn's head. Since he'd left home, he had hated Rupert Magee for what he'd done. They talked about his need to forgive and prayed about God helping him find forgiveness. All those feelings of animosity must be coming back. Once more, Quinn would have to find it in his heart to forgive with a completeness that would heal the relationship.

When Quinn found out that Rupert and Elizabeth owned the farm next to his parents, he insisted on going over by himself. "I have to settle this thing with Rupert." He pulled Kathleen into his arms in the privacy of the bedroom they'd been given. "I trust my parents' and Elizabeth's judgment, but I have to make amends with Rupert myself."

"I understand." Kathleen breathed in Quinn's familiar scent, contentment wrapping around her. Exhaustion made her weak.

"I want you to rest while I'm gone." Quinn put his hand over her rounded belly. "Carrying this little one is tiring without all the traveling we've done. I'll tell Mom you're napping, and I'll wake you up when I get back." He put her in bed and kissed her before leaving. Kathleen drifted off, praying everything would be settled in a peaceful manner.

⁂

Lord, You have to help me here. I'm so new at this forgiveness. I've harbored ill feelings toward Rupert for so long, I'm not sure I know how to truly forgive. Help me do that, Jesus, and show me right from the start that he's truly changed. Quinn nudged his horse to a faster walk as he finished praying. Peace settled over him as the buildings of Elizabeth and Rupert's place came in sight. The hollow knock of an axe chopping wood reverberated in the air.

Pulling his horse to a stop, Quinn sat at the edge of the yard taking in the neat, welcoming appearance of the property. This didn't resemble the Magee's disorderly home at all. He could see Elizabeth's happiness in the bright flowers along the house. He could also see a caring man's touch in the well-mended fences and tall woodpile ready for winter.

Swinging down from the horse, Quinn stepped up on the

porch. The door flew open, and his sister flung herself into his arms. "Quinn, I can't believe you're here. I've missed you so much."

He held her away and looked at her. Cupping her cheek, he fought the emotion clogging his throat. "It's been a long time, Sis."

The door creaked open once more. Quinn's hold on his sister tightened for a moment, then relaxed. He looked up and met Rupert's hesitant gaze. This wasn't the braggart he'd fought so long ago. Quinn could see this was a man at peace with himself and God. Rupert Magee, one-time bully and braggart, exuded compassion.

"Afternoon, Rupert." Quinn held out his hand.

"Quinn." Rupert's large hand engulfed Quinn's. There wasn't a contest of wills, as Quinn would have once had. Instead, a feeling of utter peace seemed to flow between them. Elizabeth took her husband's hand, concern furrowing her brow.

"I hear we're brothers in more ways than one." Quinn grinned as Rupert raised his eyebrow. "Last fall I became a Christian. That makes us brothers through marriage and through the Lord. Welcome to the family."

Rupert's eyes glittered with moisture. Tears ran down Elizabeth's cheeks. Quinn stepped forward, and the two men enfolded Elizabeth in a long-awaited hug.

ஃ

Voices and the delicious smell of roasted meat woke Kathleen. She could tell from the shadows that evening approached. The bedroom door swung open, and Quinn peeked in.

"Awake at last?" He crossed to the bed and kissed her. "My sister is here. You have to meet her."

Kathleen stretched and swung her legs off the bed. "How's Rupert?" She tried to keep the question light.

"He's great with my sister." A rueful smile quirked Quinn's lips. "Once more, I see where God's hand was at work when I couldn't understand. He used Elizabeth's godly response to Rupert's meanness to eat at him until he yielded his life. They make a wonderful couple and are even talking about taking a trip to Tucson to visit us in a year or two."

Fixing her hair, Kathleen couldn't help putting her hand over the birthmark on her cheek. Quinn's parents hadn't said a word, but she knew they noticed. How could anyone not see the mark?

Quinn's hands settled on her shoulders. He brushed a kiss on her neck, sending a tingle down her spine. "You are so beautiful, my love. Come meet my sister, and you'll understand a lot."

Hand in hand, they walked into the kitchen, where Mary and Elizabeth were visiting. A tiny baby slept in a cradle in the corner.

"Here she is." Mary beamed at Kathleen. "Your new sister."

A young woman as tiny as Mary with wheat-colored hair turned to greet Kathleen. Her eyes were a darker blue than Quinn's. Her smile radiated joy. Kathleen's throat became tight. Her eyes burned. She could feel Quinn's arms tighten around her as she gazed at his sister, a beautiful girl with a dark brown birthmark staining her left cheek.

"Kathleen, I'm so happy to meet you." Elizabeth came forward and opened her arms. Kathleen stepped into her embrace. No wonder Quinn hadn't looked at her star as a deformity. He'd grown up with a sister with a mark like hers. Now she understood all his comments about Elizabeth being tormented and teased. That's why he'd been so drawn to her and so protective of her.

"Is this my new sister-in-law?" The deep voice boomed across the kitchen. Elizabeth released Kathleen and turned to the huge man standing beside her father. He came over and wrapped an arm around Elizabeth, love and gentleness radiating from him. "I hear you're visiting from the great Sonoran Desert."

"That's right." Quinn slipped his arms around her. "Rupert, I'd like you to meet Kathleen, my Sonoran Star." He leaned around and kissed her on the cheek.

Joy such as she'd never thought possible filled Kathleen.

A Letter To Our Readers

Dear Reader:

In order that we might better contribute to your reading enjoyment, we would appreciate your taking a few minutes to respond to the following questions. We welcome your comments and read each form and letter we receive. When completed, please return to the following:

Rebecca Germany, Fiction Editor
Heartsong Presents
PO Box 719
Uhrichsville, Ohio 44683

1. Did you enjoy reading *Sonoran Star* by Nancy J. Farrier?
   ❏ Very much! I would like to see more books
      by this author!
   ❏ Moderately. I would have enjoyed it more if

   _____

   _____

   _____

2. Are you a member of **Heartsong Presents**? Yes ❏ No ❏
   If no, where did you purchase this book?_____

   _____

3. How would you rate, on a scale from 1 (poor) to 5 (superior), the cover design?_____

4. On a scale from 1 (poor) to 10 (superior), please rate the following elements.

   _____ Heroine   _____ Plot

   _____ Hero   _____ Inspirational theme

   _____ Setting   _____ Secondary characters

5. These characters were special because _____
   _____
   _____

6. How has this book inspired your life? _____
   _____
   _____

7. What settings would you like to see covered in future
   Heartsong Presents books? _____
   _____
   _____

8. What are some inspirational themes you would like to see
   treated in future books? _____
   _____
   _____

9. Would you be interested in reading other **Heartsong
   Presents** titles?   Yes ❑   No ❑

10. Please check your age range:
    ❑ Under 18   ❑ 18-24   ❑ 25-34
    ❑ 35-45   ❑ 46-55   ❑ Over 55

Name _____

Occupation _____

Address _____

City _____ State _____ Zip _____

Email _____

China Tapestry

An exotic setting for ageless love. Woven through all things are vibrant threads of love—the love of God to His creation, the love of a parent to a child, the love of a man to a woman. Experience that love, enriching the fabric of life, against the backdrop of vivid Chinese culture.

paperback, 352 pages, 5 ³⁄₁₆" x 8"

·······Presents·······

Great Inspirational Romance at a Great Price!

Heartsong Presents books are inspirational romances in contemporary and historical settings, designed to give you an enjoyable, spiritlifting reading experience. You can choose wonderfully written titles from some of today's best authors like Peggy Darty, Sally Laity, Tracie Peterson, Colleen L. Reece, Lauraine Snelling, and many others.

When ordering quantities less than twelve, above titles are $2.95 each.
Not all titles may be available at time of order.

Hearts♥ng Presents
Love Stories Are Rated G!

That's for godly, gratifying, and of course, great! If you love a thrilling love story but don't appreciate the sordidness of some popular paperback romances, **Heartsong Presents** is for you. In fact, **Heartsong Presents** is the *only inspirational romance book club* featuring love stories where Christian faith is the primary ingredient in a marriage relationship.

Sign up today to receive your first set of four never-before-published Christian romances. Send no money now; you will receive a bill with the first shipment. You may cancel at any time without obligation, and if you aren't completely satisfied with any selection, you may return the books for an immediate refund!

Imagine. . .four new romances every four weeks—two historical, two contemporary—with men and women like you who long to meet the one God has chosen as the love of their lives. . .all for the low price of $9.97 postpaid.

To join, simply complete the coupon below and mail to the address provided. **Heartsong Presents** romances are rated G for another reason: They'll arrive *Godspeed!*